Baptized in Her Seduction:

A Church Love Affair 2

Written By Olivia Shaw

DISCARDED
From Nashville Public Library

Baptized in Her Seduction: A Church Love Affair 2
© 2017 by Olivia Shaw
Published by Kindred Soul Publication
All rights reserved. This book or any portion thereof may not be reproduced or used in any manner whatsoever without the express written permission of the publisher except for the use of brief quotations in a book review. This book is a work of fiction. Names, characters, places, and incidents either are the product of the author's imagination or are used fictitiously and are not to be construed as real. Any resemblance to actual persons, living or dead, business establishments, events, or locales is purely coincidental.

Acknowledgements

I am so thankful for life, salvation, my family and friends, my church, my mind, the mobility of my limbs, my career, car, health, and everything in between! Lord, You are so good. Thank You for my gift. I pray that everyone who reads my work would be blessed and encouraged, and would be inspired to know You better. Although this is a work of fiction, Lord, You will receive the honor! You will be praised, celebrated, and glorified with every word! Continue to use me through my words and my life. Amen.

A special thank you to my parents, Mark and Tammy Shaw, and sister Tiffany. Thank you for all of your love, encouragement, and support. I appreciate you more than you will ever know! I pray that I continue to make you proud with every book and every positive choice that I make. Love you!

To Paris, my best friend and love of my life: I will soon be Mrs. Reel and I'm so excited about it! #ReelLove

To my Kindred Soul Publications pen sisters and brothers, readers, supporters, and friends: you ALL inspire and encourage me with every purchase, rating, review, and book release. Stephani Mickens and Drusilla Mars: I love you ladies for LIFE! Thank you for the opportunities you've provided for my career.

To my pastors, Robert Pyles and Auntie/Patricia Clayton, and the entire Abundant Faith Church of Integrity family as well as my Milwaukee Youth Falcons family: thank you, thank you, thank you for everything! Your love and support means everything to me and I absolutely do not take it for granted!

To all my Christian Fiction readers and supporters: thank you for your support! Sometimes my work may rub people the WRONG way because of its content (i.e., promiscuous pastors, adulterous elders, etc.); however, I will be the first to say I was not always saved. I did not always act and think Christ-like, and my fiction reflects that. I gave my life to God at seventeen years old, and since then, have seen so many things within the church (not my church specifically)—good and bad. My stories reflect real-life situations; these are situations that people can relate to or identify with. I apologize if I have offended anyone by my stories, but know that we are saved by God's amazing grace. We are all redeemed of our pasts and transgressions, and no one is without imperfections. It's time we stop pretending to be above everyone else and exude love for all walks of life.

As fellow Christians and servants of the Most High, understand that my job is to bring souls to CHRIST. Most of us were sinners and "in the world," and have testimonies that will blow the world's minds! So why then, when I write about certain situations is it a problem? Why is my fiction work a reflection of me as a Christian? If Bishop T.D. Jakes had written the same book, would it be perceived as unGodly as well?

I am not attempting to please man with my Christian fiction—know that. My desire is to meet people (believers and non-believers) where they are;

I wish to provide hope and encouragement, and to allow them to get to know the Father and how all mistakes and sins can be made perfect in HIM. That's the ultimate goal. So despite some of the disheartening reviews I've gotten about being a disgrace to the Christian community, may God bless you, and I thank you anyhow for purchasing or reading my work. Pray for me and my mission! It's still ALL love! *-Sincerely, Olivia*

Prologue

Previously in "Baptized in Her Seduction: A Church Love Affair"...

"Baby, wake up."

"Hmm?" Lorraina stirred awake from her deep slumber and glanced up. Jhalil was hovered over her as he whispered. The room smelled of cologne as he moved around and continued to get ready for the day. She assumed he was heading either to a corporate breakfast, or to a church meeting, by the way he was dressed.

"I'm headed out. I should be no more than an hour or so. I'll call you on my way home," he said and kissed her forehead.

"Okay. See you, baby." Lorraina smiled and watched him walk out.

He winked and then closed the door behind him. He was handsome as ever and outfitted in a black shirt and black slacks. A dark grey and black pinstriped suit jacket was draped over his forearm.

He accessorized with black diamonds across his wrist and a black matte tungsten pinky ring.

All night, he had tossed and turned. Each time that she asked him if he was okay, he would simply say that he was thinking. She knew their discussion yesterday probably was weighing heavily on his mind, but he would never admit it. Lorraina hated that she had brought the added stress to his life, but it was better to get things out now than later.

His scent lingered even after an hour later, when she text him about his whereabouts. She started on breakfast and was whipping up the batter to pancakes when she received a text. It was Jhalil telling her he would be another fifteen minutes or so. She poured the thick, buttery batter into the sizzling pan with a grin.

"Thank You, God. Things could have went left, but they didn't," Lorraina said into the atmosphere.

In her petite hands, she prepared each plate, neatly folded the napkins, and placed silverware next to each plate. She took a quick, relaxing shower, and then waited for him with two glasses of pulp-free orange juice. She tried not to watch the clock too much.

Meanwhile, across town…

"Hi, can I start you fellas off with anything to drink?"

Jhalil looked up from the menu and knew that only water was his idea of a breakfast, at least until he made it back to Lorraina. His mind was focused on bigger, more important things. Although a prayer breakfast was going on currently, he could not help but to stare down the obnoxiously smug negro directly across from him.

Of course, as fate always had it, he was in the room with Curt at possibly the worst time in history. After all, Jhalil's blood was already still seething from what Lorraina had revealed to him. He knew that he was not ready to address the issue with Curt personally, but seeing him now, made

Jhalil rethink the situation. The more he sat across from him, he thought of how he could have touched Lorraina. Jhalil hated that his hands had stroked and massaged his woman once upon a time. Jhalil grew angrier and angrier at the fact that someone else's lips had skimmed over Lorraina's. It was sickening.

"Uh, Pastor Jhalil?" one of the ministers cleared his throat and asked cautiously. "You okay over there? Did you want anything to eat?"

He rolled his neck around and stretched his back. Then he sat up straighter in his seat and shook his head. He took his eyes off of Curt and then rubbed his forehead. "No, I'm good. Can we, uh, wrap this up? I have to speak with Brother Curt in private, please."

"But Pastor, we just got here not long ago…"

"What did I say?" Jhalil snapped and then calmed down some. He noticed the look on everybody's faces while he cleared his throat and then stood up. "Excuse me while I run to the little boy's room."

Silence followed him as he entered the restroom not far away. Jhalil sighed and leaned against the wall. He did not really have to pee, but he did need to keep it cool until he could figure everything out. Perhaps today wouldn't be the best time to give Curt a piece of his mind.

Jhalil checked his phone as it buzzed. It was Lorraina texting him again. She sent a picture of herself making pouty lips at him as if to say she was lonely. Then, not even a second later, she sent another text.

Missing you…come home soon! Food's getting cold.

Even miles away, she knew just what he needed. Jhalil smirked and found peace in the fact that she was craving his presence. He decided to just leave, whether the men were done with their meeting or not. As he turned to exit the restroom, the door opened and Curt entered.

Jhalil faked a grin and nodded. "Have a good day."

"You good, pastor? You've been so short with me today."

Jhalil closed his eyes and exhaled. He did not care if it came off as rude. He was exactly four steps away from the door and was about fifty steps from reaching the outside of the restaurant. Curt had likely come in on purpose to antagonize him. Lord knows he didn't want to go to jail today, but…

"Did I do something wrong, the reason you wanted to speak to me in private?" Curt continued. His voice was so innocent, but Jhalil knew the truth. "Was it me poppin' up yesterday unannounced?"

"Naw. I just have a little headache," Jhalil mumbled. He never turned around and instead, reached for the door handle. "We'll discuss it another day, man."

"Maybe a little sex will help?" Curt inquired and fumbled with his bowtie in the mirror. "I heard sex eases stress, headaches, pain, and all that jazz."

"Oh yeah?" Jhalil responded dryly, "Have a good day."

"If I had a woman as sexy as Lorraina," Curt said cockily and slowly, "I'd be at home with her now, instead of at a prayer meeting. I mean, with thighs like that, and a booty so round? You could not PAY me to leave that fine piece of tail."

Jhalil whipped around and just knew some hidden camera crew was pranking him. His breath caught in his throat as he attempted to find the best way to handle it. *What would Jesus do?* He asked himself. That thought was short-lived as Curt continued to speak.

"I mean, seriously, bruh. You really thought I came around to help you with your little startup ministry? I just wanted to taste your first lady one last time. She was so good before that I couldn't help myself."

Jesus would have to work a miracle...*now*. Jhalil lost control and forcefully shoved Curt into the mirror, breaking it instantly. Shards of glass flew everywhere as he grabbed Curt's neck with one hand, and then punched him with the other hand. Curt's nose became bloodied, and then he took a punch at Jhalil.

"After all I've done, you want to *fight* me?" Curt asked as if he did not realize why Jhalil was so mad. "Bruh, come on! Let me go! You—you broke my nose!"

The door behind them opened, and in rushed another member of the clergy. "Hey! Hey! Cut it out, guys!" The man attempted to break them apart, but their bubbling anger and relentless adrenaline kept the scuffle going.

A worker burst through the doors shortly after. It was a woman who held a phone up to her ear. She screamed at the men who were moving around in the restroom violently. "I've called the police! They're on the way! Stop before you kill yourselves!"

Jhalil was the first to back away and spit his saliva at Curt. Although Curt was much more towering and huskier, Jhalil was quicker on his feet. He shook his sore knuckles out that were beginning to bleed badly, and then he wiped the corner of his nose where he was not sure if it were blood or mucus flowing from it.

"You thought I was going to keep quiet about you wrapping up her panties? I don't care what kind of relationship you used to have with her. You stay away from Lorraina! You stay away from *me*!" Jhalil yelled and kicked Curt a final time.

The once smug man was now lying on the floor in a growing puddle of blood. He looked helpless as he attempted to catch his breath and make sense of the beating his body had just endured. Jhalil limped away and rubbed at his neck. The female worker jumped back in horror.

"You don't need to call the police. Just call a plastic surgeon. Bruh may need his face reconstructed."

Jhalil looked back at Curt a final time and walked out.

When he arrived home, Lorraina had fallen back to sleep on the couch. Their uneaten breakfast was still on the table. A part of him felt horrible for missing out on her delicious home cooking after she slayed over the stove, but the other part of him felt relieved. He had literally beaten and taken his frustrations out on Curt and it felt good.

He sat down a few feet from Lorraina on the opposite loveseat with his head down. God was likely not pleased with his actions but he could not help it. Curt had made some over-the-top remarks and it had gotten him a black eye, swollen jaw, and possible broken nose. Jhalil was no longer the pastor with rational thinking. He was the overprotective fiancé looking out for his woman, and he would do it all over again.

Lorraina stirred awake beside him and yawned. As she stretched, she opened her eyes completely and then screamed in shock. She was no doubt surprised to see him sitting there, but was probably also alarmed by his bloody shirt, erratic breathing, and unruly appearance.

"What happened? Are you okay?"

"The better question is: do you forgive me for keeping you waiting?"

"Of course," she said and looked him up and down. Any sleep that had been tugging at her seemed to disappear immediately. "Don't tell me. You got into it with Curt?"

"It was a little discussion, that's all."

"More like a BRAWL! I'm so sorry you felt like you had to defend my honor in this way. Are you sure you're okay? Let me see your face."

"Baby, I'm fine." He dodged her hands when she reached for him. "That guy is an idiot. He won't be bothering you ever again, you hear me?"

She nodded and got up to get him a washcloth. "I hear you. So that's *his* blood?"

"Yeah." Jhalil followed behind her and pulled his shirt off. He tossed it on the hardwood floor and then his voice took on a playful tone. "I'm just ready to shower and eat. Reheat my food, woman, and I'm not going to ask again."

"Whatever you say, Mr. Harrison," she joked, but at the back of her mind, she was upset that he had gotten hurt because of her. She and her baggage was always coming back to haunt her and the people she loved, and she had the craziest feeling that Curtis was not even close to being finished.

Chapter One

"You must've seen what I was wearing tonight?"

Lorraina looked up from applying lotion to her arms and admired Jhalil's outfit. He wore a getup that matched hers in color and in fabric. They both were dressed to impress and ready for their night on the town. He rocked a cream cashmere pullover, tan slacks, and tan loafers. She also wore a cream blouse, a chocolate brown pencil skirt, and tan and chocolate brown wedge sandals. They were coordinated perfectly. Earlier in the week, he promised to show her a good time since they had not gotten any alone time lately, and she was anxious to begin their date. They vowed that they would put all the phones, watches, iPods, iPads, and any other distractions away.

Tonight was theirs simply because as of late, life had gotten chaotic but beautiful.

The ministry was officially a thing of the future, and many people were pouring in by the numbers every Sunday and Tuesday evening. It was like the personification of Deuteronomy 30, because God had surely restored everything that was lost. Jhalil was preaching the Good Word as if he had done it for years, and Lorraina was his faithful first lady and touching women's lives all over with her testimony. A few of the nosey church mothers loved to turn their nose up at her, given her past. Their relationship was often questioned as well. After all, a male and female heading a church as anything other than a married couple was almost unheard of. Lorraina was determined to move forward from the naysayers and let God handle the rest. She was not going to let those moments define her any longer.

Nothing or no one could stop her spiritual "resurrection," just as nothing or no one could stop the budding love that Jhalil had for her. He had mentioned it again and again about a simple wedding ceremony, but Lorraina was convinced that when the time was right, their nuptials would be in order. There was just so much to be concerned with lately, including providing for their four-year old foster child whom they had taken in.

A member of their clergy—a young, drug-addicted mother—had become overwhelmed and needed help with her son so Jhalil had volunteered their home temporarily. Lorraina would joke that he favored Jhalil in many ways and ask if he was really the father, but he would only laugh it off.

She could honestly say she never imagined being thrown into motherhood this way, but it was God's Will, and she would stick to it as best as she could. She enjoyed loving and protecting a little person. His name was Noah and he had the sweetest spirit and temperament she had ever seen from a child. He had been dropped off an hour ago to her best friend, Terreana's, house.

"Maybe. Maybe not," she joked with a wink.

Jhalil approached her with his arms open and she fell into his embrace with a smile. He smelled amazing, and looked incredible. He had completely reinvented his look, and wore a low-cut now. He had grown out his beard as well, so it was nice and full now so that each time they kissed, it tickled her face.

"You ready?"

"I am," she responded and tucked her ALDO clutch purse under an arm.

They were heading to a jazz festival that took place every year in Dunges Bay Park. Lorraina was a huge music lover, and Jhalil had played several instruments as a child. This date would definitely be one for the books.

He brought along an oversized lawn chair and a thick fleece blanket that he placed over both of their shoulders. They had front row seats to the musicians, and the show was just getting started as they settled down in the grass. Lorraina nestled closer to him; she was half on his lap, and half on the chair. His arm wrapped around her hips and held her in place.

They enjoyed music and refreshments for more than an hour before the band took the stage for their final song. The lead singer of the group stepped forward and looked around at the crowd.

"Y'all are some beautiful, groovy people out there! Give it up for yourselves tonight," he said into the microphone. He was obviously still stuck in the seventies, judging from his wardrobe, hairstyle, and lingo.

Lorraina smirked and looked around. There was so much love in the air. There were mainly couples that had come out tonight. The atmosphere was different; she could not quite put her finger on it, but even Jhalil was different. He wore a continuous smile on his face and he could not stop looking at her. She knew she looked great, but his stare made her feel like the prettiest girl in the world.

"From my understanding, I have a friend here tonight who has an important mission. He wants to propose to his girlfriend," the musician continued. "Where are you, buddy?"

Lorraina nudged Jhalil and looked around to see whom the musician was referring to. To her surprise, the spotlight swung around and stopped on them. Lorraina jumped in surprise and felt her mouth go dry. The crowd ooohed and aaahed, and the band played soft music while Jhalil cleared his throat and stood up. He brought her along with him and wrapped his arms around her.

"Baby, you already know how I feel about you. You've changed my life and everything in it for the better. I can't live my life without you, and I pray you feel the same," Jhalil spoke sincerely and then released her so that he could get down on one knee.

Lorraina's heart thumped as if it was a drum; she swallowed the lump in her throat. Any other woman would have been ecstatic to be in this position.

"Will you please spend the rest of your life with me? Will you marry me, Lorraina?"

The night was young and romance was in the air. The mood was just right with music and dim lighting, and the love of her life was kneeling down before her. This should have been the most beautiful time of her life and certainly the most memorable. Yet she wasn't overjoyed. She wasn't ready to say 'yes.' She knew she had underlying issues that needed resolving, and there were definitely all kinds of demons that needed slaying.

She wasn't quite ready to expose the skeletons in her closet. She knew she couldn't embarrass Jhalil in front of all of the onlookers, so with tears of frustration in her eyes, she nodded and jumped up and down. She had to take on the role of an excited, unexpected girlfriend.

"Yes! Yes, I will!" she cried out and her voice was lack of any emotion or sincerity, but Jhalil did not seem to notice.

The bandleader pumped a fist and then clapped his hands. He reminded Lorraina of the late, great James Brown with his permed hair and leather ensemble. "Let's give it up for this beautiful, young couple! They're headed to the Left Hand Club pretty soon! Woo hoo!" he announced.

The crowd roared with affirmation and excitement. Jhalil smiled and kissed her with passion, while she desperately tried to understand why she was so disconnected and torn about their future.

    That night, as they settled in their separate beds, she knew that they were still trying to head down the straight and narrow path. However, she needed a release. There was no one for her to really talk to who would understand her logic—not even Jhalil, so she went to her go-to stress reliever. Buried underneath her sheets, she took out her seven-inch, black sex toy that she kept hidden from Jhalil, and even her closest of friends. She cried herself to sleep while she pleasured herself, and cursed her own, cold heart.

Chapter Two

The next morning, Lorraina pretended to be asleep for as long as possible, until she was sure that Jhalil had left the house. It was her mission to avoid him as much as possible until she could come up with good reasoning as to why they needed to wait on marriage. Plus, she knew he would be asking her a million different questions, and talking about their wedding, and she was not ready to face him just yet. As she finally pulled herself out of bed, she searched the house for him and instead found a note on the refrigerator.

The brothers and I are meeting at the church. Here's some money to do whatever. See you later, baby. I mean FIANCEE. HAHAHAHA! Love U. -J

She read his note with a saddened heart and admired her ring finger. He had great taste and had picked out a gorgeous ring that fit her style perfectly. But it still just wasn't right. She took the money he left and stashed it in her purse, and then showered and got Noah ready for the day. She would shop away her pain, beginning with retail, and ending with groceries.

More than an hour later, she found herself in the crowded aisles of Pick N' Save. She spoke aloud to herself about what they needed for the next week and a half. Noah looked at her now with big, bright eyes as he sat in the front part of a shopping cart. He was probably wondering if she had lost her mind. Honey Dijon chicken wraps had been on her mind to make today, so she made sure she had all of the ingredients. She picked up things she had no business buying, and grabbed more than enough food.

As she headed down one aisle in particular, she baby-talked to Noah. He had a hearing impairment and wore a cochlear implant. He studied her lips, burst into laughter, and then continued to smile at her as she spoke.

"We're just about ready to go. I just need one more thing, okay, man?" she told him and squinted while she read the nutrition label on a can of black beans.

"I didn't know you were a mother."

Lorraina glanced up from the can. It was Curt. Like all villains to any story, they just had to keep reappearing and making the good people's lives miserable. She sighed and placed the box on the shelf. That was her cue to leave this store.

"There's a lot of things you don't know about me," she said simply.

"It's been seven months. You should be thankful."

She glanced over a shoulder. "Thankful? And why is that?"

He looked at a can of lima beans, and she knew it was to irk her. There was no way that he could be shopping for those types of beans. No black man in America *willingly* shopped for lima beans.

"I could have pressed charges. I could have gotten your man arrested. I could have done a lot to ruin your name and good graces."

"So why didn't you?" she challenged and turned completely.

Curt shook his head thoughtfully. He glanced at her body and lingered on her legs. She was dressed modestly in flared jeans and a lengthy blouse that hung past her buttocks. Even still, Lorraina felt like he was undressing her with his eyes. Finally, he rubbed the patch of hair along his jawline and then shrugged.

"It's all very simple. I really liked you, Lorraina," he spoke seriously. "You *played* me, and I'm not going to lie. It hurt a lot."

"I'm sorry, Curtis. What more do you want me to say? I made a horrible mistake but I had no idea it would turn into anything more than a good time."

"Just say you'll go out for one day with me. Nothing more and nothing less. I won't press the issue anymore, and I won't give you a hard time. I won't even come around anymore if you agree to it. Just give me one final night."

"Please don't do this." She could feel Noah's eyes on her in confusion. He could sense her anxiety as she balled her fists against the cart rail.

"Nothing sexual. Just a simple date," Curt said firmly.

Lorraina could not be too sure if his intentions were good or not. She studied his body language and he did not seem like he was high off of anything but his ego. It unnerved her that she was even considering going with him.

"Why are you doing this?" she asked.

"Just say yes. I promise it's nothing like that. Just…a…simple…date," he repeated as if she had not heard him the first few times.

"When? Where?"

Curt smiled as if he had just been gifted the world.

"Meet me at that new restaurant that just opened up downtown. Six thirty. Don't keep me waiting."

"Whatever." She turned away from his smug grin and looked to Noah who was still just as confused about this strange man speaking with his guardian. "You ready to go, baby?"

He nodded, understanding her, and then kicked his little legs in glee. If only he knew what she had foolishly agreed to. Now she had to figure out what she was going to tell Jhalil tomorrow. In a matter of seconds, her life had gotten that much more complicated and she hated herself for even doing something so stupid.

***

Of course, time flew by quicker than she had ever experienced in her life and it was time to meet Curt at the destination he chose. She had never heard of this restaurant, but there were rave reviews about it online. It was situated in the middle of other thriving businesses, and looked to be bustling with food connoisseurs. She made up a lie to tell to Jhalil, and he surprisingly was nonchalant about her request to have a night out with the girls. He even told her to stay out as long as possible.

That was odd. He usually reprimanded her for hanging out with her friends because of their pasts and current affairs with married men. She was the only one of her crew to turn her life around so he wanted her to stay as far away as she could from those women. He especially wanted her to be careful now that she was representing his ministry. But tonight, something was different about him.

Lorraina shimmied the ruby-colored dress up her hips and then turned with her back to him to zip.

"You look incredible. Is this new?"

"No. You've just never seen it before."

"And where did you say you were going again?"

"The lounge on Fourth Street—Mickey's."

"Have fun." He nodded in thought and studied the side of her face. Worry was etched all over her expression so he just had to ask. "Is something wrong?"

Lorraina said nothing and concentrated on smoothing down the tiny hairs along her forehead.

She wore a simple ponytail that had been fluffed with a comb to give her extra volume. On her lips was a nude-colored lipstick that brought out the yellow undertones in her skin. She felt attractive, but all for the wrong reasons. There were no true motives as to why she was going out with a man who could ruin everything for her with a simple phone call.

She arrived to the restaurant without successfully talking herself out of the foolishness.

"Hi, I am here for…"

The maître d' interrupted her words. "Ah, yes. The gentleman informed us that you would be arriving shortly. Right this way, madam."

Lorraina followed the petite Asian woman to the back of the restaurant. A private room awaited her, which she was grateful for. This meant that they would be hidden from view from any nosey onlookers. She could not afford to be caught dining out with anyone other than Jhalil, and certainly not with Curt. That would be a bad look altogether.

He was nowhere in sight as she settled in one of the loveseats and exhaled.

"Why did I agree to this?" she questioned aloud.

There was an uneasy feeling in her heart that she could not shake. There was no telling what kind of game Curt was playing but she knew that she was desperate for some kind of resolution. If having dinner with him helped her get rid of him from here on out, then she would be satisfied.

She waited fourteen minutes exactly before declaring that her time was wasted. But as she stood up and reached for her handbag, another hand closed around her wrist.

"You leavin' *already*?" a voice pondered with sarcasm.

The warmth of Curt's breath tickled the tiny hairs at the back of her neck. A chill ran down her spine and seemed to run throughout her body. Finally, the chill went to her feet where her toes curled, but not in a good way. She faced him and was shocked to find that they were not the only two in the room. Two other men, dressed in freshly steamed suits, accompanied Curt. They wore black shades and earpieces as if they were a part of the Secret Service.

"What is *this*?"

He noticed her face and held up his hands. "Calm down. Calm down. These are just a couple friends of mine, Emilio and Julio. We're here to talk with you and enjoy a little Italian cuisine. We're not trying to start any trouble, okay?"

She was still unsure about all of this; the way Emilio looked at her up and down unnerved her. Even behind his dark-colored shades, she had managed to capture his attention. Perhaps she should not have worn such a revealing, form fitting dress. The men practically *searched* through the chiffon material of her dress for skin and whatever else they could find.

As she reluctantly sat back down, she breathed out a deep exhale. Whatever was to become of this night, she did not necessarily care.

She simply wanted everything to be over so she could head back home to relax in her warm bed.

"I'm glad you came with me today. I promise, I won't keep you all night, and I won't be inappropriate."

Lorraina studied his expression. He seemed genuine in his statements. She spoke over the soft music overhead, "Well, I appreciate that."

"What will you be having?" Curt asked and peered over his menu at her.

She shrugged. "I'm not even sure. I'm not a big Italian fan."

"Word? That's new to my ears. So, what do you normally eat?"

"Anything that comes from my own kitchen," she joked. "Soul food…Creole dishes…Jamaican cuisine."

He nodded thoughtfully. "You cook?"

"Why is that so surprising? Most women *do*, don't they?"

"Not the ones I've dated," he admitted and rubbed the patch of hair along his jawline. "It's like pulling teeth with some of these twenty-first century women. They don't want to cook, clean, work, or anything else. They just want a man to do it all, and expect him not to tire out. *Please*."

"What kind of women were YOU dating?" Lorraina chuckled and placed her menu down beside her on the table. "All of the women in my family and around me were brought up with totally different views. But hey, to each her own."

The waitress came around and took their orders. Emilio and Julio sat at the opposite end of the table and conversed amongst themselves. She was content because that made things a little less awkward.

"If you don't mind me asking," he began to say, but she cut him off.

"I mind. Anytime somebody starts a sentence like that, it's a personal question."

Curt laughed and looked surprised at her wittiness. "It's not like that. Well, it is, but you don't have to answer if you don't want." He paused and looked her directly in the eye. "Are you in love with Jhalil?"

Lorraina swallowed hard. On one hand, she could be honest with him because he genuinely seemed interested. On the other hand, she was unsure of where this information would be used.

"Why do you want to know?"

"I'm just curious."

"What? You're going to run and tell him what I say? Who's benefitting from this piece of information?"

"My goodness. *Chill*. You're so defensive, Lo Lo. I'm merely just making conversation. Didn't I say I didn't want to start any trouble with you? I only wanted to have a nice dinner where we could talk."

"First of all, do *not* call me Lo Lo, and two, yes I love him. He knows that already."

Curt shrugged and nodded. "See? That wasn't so bad, was it? That's all I wanted to know."

Lorraina continued to stare at him. Things grew quiet but she kept her gaze on him, even while the waitress came with their plates and placed them on the table. The food looked delicious and steamed from the oven still. Only when her mouth began to water at the aromas of flavor did she look away from him.

"What now? I know that wasn't all you wanted to know. Don't play with me."

"No one's playing with you…this time," Curt paused and a snide smile tugged at the corners of his mouth. She could slap it off. "Now, several months ago? I played with you in more ways than one. That was a playground that I would not mind frequenting again."

It was obvious that he was referring to her body, and the few times that they had fooled around. She sighed because she knew the shaming and name-calling would be next. This was probably his plan all along.

"Okay, you know what? You're crossing the line!" Her voice rose as she stood to her feet for the second time. Her napkin fell to the floor from her lap. "I'm leaving!"

"You might not want to do that." His voice was controlled and low. He never faltered as he leaned to bite into his steak. "You might see something you don't like."

"Oh, like seeing you is any better? What can be worse? Goodbye, Curt…for good. I don't care what you do from here on out. I can't put myself through this anymore."

"Okay. Go ahead, sweetheart."

Lorraina snatched her bag from the table and stepped through the doors separating the private room from the restaurant's main seating area. She mumbled under her breath in irritation and half expected Curt to come up behind her to try to stop her. But he never came. Instead, she was stopped literally in her tracks at the sight of Jhalil, who had encouraged her to stay out late and have a good time, seated in the corner of the restaurant.

Her handbag dropped with a gentle thud, and her knees seemed to lock in place. She was not upset because he was out having dinner nor was she mad that he wanted to enjoy himself and dress up with a suit and tie. What upset her was that Jhalil was out having dinner, dressed like a GQ model, and sitting across from another woman.

    This bastard was cheating while she tried desperately to save her family from Curt's foolish games.

Chapter Three

Jhalil chuckled and grabbed the cloth napkin from the table as Lorraina continued to look on in shock. He seemed genuinely happy and then reached over to wipe the young woman's face free of pasta sauce. Her heart sank a little more in her chest; it was darn near on top of her feet. They literally looked like a couple in love.

The woman, from what Lorraina could see, was attractive, petite, and honey complexioned. Her smooth skin was free of any makeup, except for the light splash of blush. Either it was blush on her cheeks, or Jhalil had her blushing nonstop. She could not decipher. Lorraina's perusal took in the woman's wardrobe; she wore a simple black dress, fishnet stockings with bows on the backs of each ankle, and black kitten heels. Lastly, her thick hair was naturally curly and pinned up intricately. The woman was stunning.

"What…what did you do, Jhalil?" she asked into the atmosphere.

Tears brimmed her eyes. She vowed that she would not make a scene nor would she allow the tears to fall from her eyes. Rapidly, she blinked away the feeling of despair that crept into her veins. She was being cheated on with a man she loved and wanted to someday marry. It was truly the slap of the century.

As she turned to leave the restaurant, a hand closed around her wrist and stopped her in her tracks. She looked up at Curt who had a knowing look on his face. Was this the very thing that he was trying to stop her from seeing? He seemed concerned by the tears welling up in her eyes, and pulled her into his arms. He leaned to kiss the top of her head, and then ushered them in the opposite direction and away from Jhalil's line of view.

"What is that? You KNEW about this?"

"Shh. Sit down. Let me talk to you for a second," Curt said and pulled the chair out for her. Only after she sat down did he continue to talk. "I didn't want you to find out this way."

"That's a load of crap and you know it, Curt. Why else would you invite me here? You knew he was coming here for whatever reason, and you wanted me to find out. I'm going to ask for the last time before I leave; what kind of game are y'all playing?"

"I'm not playing *any* game. I promise you, sweetheart. I was only trying to open your eyes to what Jhalil is really about," he said and then looked around. "Hey, Emilio! Julio!"

The two burly men walked over. "Yeah, boss?"

"Tell her what I do for a living."

They looked at Curt, then to each other, and then back to Curt again. Emilio spoke up this time. There was hesitation in his voice.

"For real, *for real*?"

"Yes. For real, *for real*. We can trust that she won't say a thing. Isn't that right, Lorraina?"

She nodded in confusion and looked back and forth between the three. When she spoke, her voice was raspy with terror, "Your secret's safe with me but…but what's going on?"

Emilio cleared his throat and crossed his arms. "We're all undercover special agents."

"What? I didn't do anything…" she began to protest with her hands up.

"No, no. It's not you we're looking out for," Curtis assured her and kept his voice low. He nodded towards the outside of the restaurant. "It's Jhalil who we've been pursuing for a few years."

This was all a shock to Lorraina as she gripped a hand over her chest. "A few years? For *what*?"

"We have reason to believe he's been participating in the sex trafficking industry."

Now, it was time for her to *really* gasp and find the ability to breathe properly. If she had not been sitting, she would have surely fallen backward. She could not believe what she was hearing.

"Please tell me this is an unfunny, sick, and long, drawn-out joke."

Emilio and Julio dismissed themselves.

"I wish I could," Curt said. "There was no other way for me to tell you, but to tell you the truth. Now, I could totally lose my job over this—Emilio and Julio included. But we're trusting that you would help us to move this assignment further. Not only that, but I cared about you enough to show you what your man *really* thought of you. He's a clown, Lorraina, and you deserve better."

"Look, all past mistakes and past relations aside. Why should I believe you? Why should I believe that this is what's really going on, and he's not just cheating on me?"

"Because of this," Curt said simply and handed her a thick, manila envelope.

She reluctantly opened the envelope with shaky hands. Much to her surprise, tucked deep in the contents of the material, were countless identification cards with Jhalil's face plastered on each one. Each card had a different name and state of residence on it. It was like the movie starring Leonardo DiCaprio, where he had posed as many different people in various professions.

She had fallen in love with a con artist. This made no sense. Why did it have to be her at the short end of the stick? Why did her heart have to be broken in this way? Perhaps it was God punishing her for all of her previous dirty deeds that she had committed while serving in the ministry. As the saying went, God didn't like ugly, and this was proof that she had been chastised because of her sins.

"Bu—but how? Why? Why would he do this?"

Curt tapped his index finger against his temple. "The mind of a criminal is a complicated one, sweetheart. All I can say is he's looking for something, whether it's love, affection, power, or control. Many of the men who seek out these women are often abusive, aggressive, and charming. Has he ever put his hands on you?"

This was a no brainer. "Well, no, but…"

"Has he ever pressured you into anything you didn't want to do?"

"Honestly, I can't say he has."

Curt nodded. "Well, you're one of the lucky ones. It's possible he does care for you, but he can't let go of the other things he's gotten himself into it. The money in this industry is addictive; it's like a drug."

Lorraina shook her head in disbelief. "So when are you guys going to convict him?"

"When we have sufficient evidence. We don't want to just go in for the kill and not have all the proper resources. That's why we need *you*. I have exhausted all of my options, and while it's pretty much against federal regulations to get a regular civilian involved, there is something about you."

Lorraina stared back at him in silence.

"You're able to get people to open up and trust every word that falls from those pretty lips. You're able to make the strongest of men fall to their knees. That's how you got me to fall so hard for you," Curt added.

Even though she was distraught because of the news she had found out, her heart warmed at his words. Maybe he wasn't so crazy after all.

"You know that cutie Noah?"

"Of course."

"Noah is the son of one of the ladies he recently met. That's another tactic for these bastards. They take the women's children and bribe them with a better life, knowing the women will do any and everything to provide for their children. This was all intentional on Jhalil's behalf."

"But she joined our church."

"Okay, and look who's leading it?"

Curt had a point.

"So, tell me something. That day we met at church…" she began to speak softly, but he held up his index finger.

"Go home now. They've received dessert, so he'll probably be leaving with the young lady, and I don't want you to run into him. Head out the back way. One of my agents will escort you. I'll be talking with you more soon, okay?"

Lorraina nodded and was still in a shock. "Okay. Thank you for this."

"Absolutely. Be safe. Keep your eyes and ears open, you hear?"

She nodded and then turned away to leave. A piece of her heart stayed right there in the restaurant as she headed home, showered, and then buried herself in her bed. Jhalil came home hours later. He settled in bed in the room next to her, and she pretended to be asleep while masking her tears in her pillows.

Life had truly been turned upside down.

Chapter Four

It was hard for Lorraina to push past the details that Curt had broken down to her, but she made a vow that if not for these women, she would fight to free Noah. Sex trafficking prevention was always something that she was passionate about. Even though she used her body willingly to lure men into her bedroom once upon a time, this was an entirely different ballpark. She had done it for satisfaction and pleasure; these women affected by sex trafficking were often tricked into the lifestyle. These women were blindsided by their companions; they were promised false hopes of riches and fulfilled dreams. This was not fair to any woman caught up in the sex trade. Lorraina vowed to do whatever it took to get Jhalil the consequences he deserved.

Call her crazy, but she was also saddened that the love of her life was leading a double life. She was sad that forever would not include them, and she was sad that she had not seen the signs earlier. But now it all made sense. Jhalil would come home with wads of money saying it was a love offering from different speaking engagements. He would always take a change of clothes with him to his outings. He would be skeptical about her accompanying him to special events. Why was she so blind to this before?

Curt was helpful in this journey. He spoke with her on many occasions, offering support, and apologizing for Jhalil's actions although it was far from his fault. She appreciated him being honest with her, just as she thanked him from opening up to her.

"How are you holding up otherwise?"

They were on the phone currently. She shrugged as if he could see her, saying, "I'm okay. I'm a little heartbroken, but I'm going to get through it like I always have."

"That's understandable. This is a man you trusted and loved. It's not going to be easy, but just from the few conversations I have had over the last several months with you, I know that you're one tough cookie. Hard interior, soft inside, and well put together."

"That was the worst analogy ever," Lorraina chuckled.

"Yeah. I couldn't backtrack once I started speaking," Curt agreed with a laugh. "What, um...what are you doing later?"

Lorraina looked over at Noah who was asleep. "I have no plans as usual."

"Is Jhalil going to be around?"

"I honestly haven't kept up with him anymore. I'm just so completely turned off from him. We've been arguing like crazy lately, and I'm so tempted to leave. If it weren't for getting Noah out of this situation, then I would have already left. He goes his way, and I go my way."

While local agents continued their investigation, she had to pretend that everything was okay. She had to smile in his face, ward off his marriage talk as politely as possible, and keep a cool head. It was hard to say the least. There was so much tension in the house that she could literally slice the air with a butter knife. Until recently, she could not fathom the thought of losing him, but now she had no choice.

"Maybe I can take you out?"

She did not hesitate. "Sure. I'll drop Noah off to my friend's house."

"You were going to ask me something a while ago when I first met with you. Do you remember what that was?"

Lorraina nodded. "It's never left my mind. I just have to know, and please, be honest with me."

"What's wrong?"

"The day you met me in church; did you know what Jhalil was doing then?"

"I knew what Jhalil was doing, yes. Like I said, we've been investigating him for a couple of years now. Did I know you two were together or had any ties? *No*. That's what complicated things once we met again. I had to put up this front and be rude to you all, and act like I was a jerk just to save face. I was happy to be reuniting with you. I can't tell you enough how attracted I was to you, so it was a blow when I found out you were dealing with him."

"How can you like someone so much that you've only met with a couple times?" she questioned.

"What's there not to like about you? You are educated, well put together, and beautiful. When I came to your church, I was looking for a place to worship, honest to God. But then my mind went other places when I saw you sitting up there with your legs crossed. The light hit your face just right; I was nearly in love!"

"Wow."

"Yeah. I'm not trying to make you uncomfortable but it was more than sex for me. Those few times we met, we talked about everything under the sun. I never believed in love at first sight, but by our fifth date, or whatever you want to call it, I really cared for you."

"This is absolutely crazy," Lorraina muttered to herself in disbelief.

She could feel her joy seeping away more and more, just as she could feel her heart breaking. All this time, she thought Curt was an idiot who wanted to destroy her reputation, relationship, and integrity, but his mission was the opposite. He was only doing those things to get as far as he could with solving this madness that Jhalil had created. She had treated him so badly. Jhalil had even fought with him.

They went to a restaurant and picked up the conversation where it had been left off.

"So where do we go from here?"

"Well, Jhalil's day is coming. I would say…"

"No, not with him. I'm talking about with us?"

"There can't be an us, can there? Certainly, with your line of work and with my involvement to Jhalil, it would never work."

"Never say never," he whispered with a wink. "As for Jhalil, my team and I are trying to hold out for another month or so. He and I will be meeting and I'm going to try to get him to confess. However, with or without the confession, we will likely have enough evidence to incriminate him by then."

"There's no way he's going to meet with you."

"Oh, but he will." He smiled. "Especially if I have money and women for him."

"What do you mean?"

"I'm going to bring in a couple of females who will pose as helpless women. We seem to have picked up on his preference. Tall, almost lanky women with light hair and petite bodies are what he's been seen with, other than the young lady we saw at the other restaurant."

"How many would you say?"

Curt thought for a moment. "Are you sure you want to know?"

"Tell me," she begged.

"More than a dozen children, and close to thirty-two women."

Lorraina grew sick to her stomach right then and there. She held a hand over her mouth but it was too late. She threw up all over the place and ran to the nearest restroom. She was sure that all attraction for her had left Curt's mind. She was a mess…literally. All eyes were on her from the other women in the restroom.

"Oh, God! Help me. This…this can't be right. This man helped me through my darkest hour. I prayed for him! How can he be this monster?" she asked aloud.

She was glad that all of the women had run off in confusion because she dropped to her knees in the stall and prayed right then and there. Never mind that it was an unsanitary place to be on her knees, she needed God right then and there. Then, after cleaning herself up, she splashed cold water on her face and looked at her image in the mirror.

She shook her head leisurely and still could not seem to wrap her mind around what had taken place. She figured this was God's punishment for all of her sins so long ago. It was either that, or she was living out one of the longest nightmares of her life.

"Just show me the truth, God. Please reveal Yourself to me."

As the words touched the atmosphere, two women walked into the restroom wearing dresses that were so short and revealing that they would make strippers blush. Their high heels clicked rhythmically against the tile, and they both settled before the mirror behind her to freshen up their lipstick.

The slimmer of the two was the first to speak. "Robyn, did you see what he had in that briefcase?"

The blonde-haired woman spoke up, "No, I didn't. What was it? He opened and closed it so quickly that I missed it."

"Giiiirl, stacks and stacks of money. That man is paid!"

"Does he think we're some kind of prostitutes or something?"

"Uh, HELLO? We are, dummy!"

"Oh, yeah! Aye, regardless, momma needs to pay the rent," the woman joked and pushed her breasts up suggestively. "Plus, he knows he's a cutie."

"He's all right. Jhalil looks *waaaay* better."

Lorraina's hands paused against the paper towel that she was using. Had this woman really said Jhalil? Her eyes looked at the women's backsides in the mirror. She took in their appearances, pieced their conversation together, and then whipped around.

"Stay far away from him."

"Huh?" Both women turned around in confusion. "You're talking to us?"

"Yes. You're here with someone named Jhalil, you said? He's brown skinned with a full beard, and on his forearm are multiple tattoos. Am I right?"

The two women looked at each other as the blonde began to talk. "Uh, yeah. That's *definitely* him. He's our date for tonight. Who are you? His wife? I swear he didn't tell us he was married! Isn't that right, Anastasia! Tell her!"

"I'm his fiancée, but that's not even my concern. My concern is that he's been involved in the sex trafficking industry and I'm trying to stop you two from falling into one of his traps. He's tricked over thirty women and several children as well. I don't want you to be the next victims."

"Are you serious right now?"

"I would not lie to you. He's under investigation as we speak. I'm here with an undercover detective now. It's best you ladies leave now. Find a back way or a side exit, but do not stop and talk to him. All he wants is your bodies and pretty faces for money. That money is for his partner to 'purchase' your freedom, so to speak. He has no idea I know everything, and he has no idea about the investigation."

Both of the women looked nervous and afraid as they nodded, picked up their handbags, and then scurried out of the restroom. Lorraina followed behind cautiously and peeked out into the restaurant. She could not see Jhalil, but she knew he was near. It was like his cologne was in the air. She returned to their table where Curt still sat and then told him what had happened.

"Did you get their names?"

"I only got their first names, Anastasia and Robyn."

"That's good enough." Curt looked around the room and then jotted the information down in his notebook. "Are you okay, by the way? Did something disagree with your stomach?"

"No, I was just overcome with emotion. That's all," she spoke hurriedly as she perused the area. "Can we leave? I don't want to chance him seeing us."

"Sure thing."

The two left and Curt dropped her back off to her home.

Chapter Five

Jhalil stood up from the booth he was seated in and walked closer to the window. Was that who he thought it was? The shape of the butt, build of the legs, and even the sway of the hips all pointed to his girlfriend. He dialed Lorraina's number but the woman he was staring down never picked up. Instead, she grabbed the man's arm that she was walking with and nestled her head against his arm. He could have sworn that was Curt and Lorraina leaving out, but obviously it wasn't. He had left her more than two hours ago to tend to business and she was asleep, so he had to have been tripping.

He turned back to the deacon that had come along with him and motioned towards the women's restroom. "Have you seen either of them leave out?"

"No, I can't say that I have, Pastor. I hope they didn't get the wrong idea."

"I hope not either. Maybe the money threw them off."

"Who knows?"

"If only they knew that I was going to pay them to stay off of the streets and get healthy," Jhalil sighed. "This mission has been hard, man. I can't even lie."

"Aren't all missions tough when you're working for Christ?"

"Yeah, but this one especially is difficult because I want to save as many women and children as possible, but there's no real support. How many pastors do you know that are out on the streets, putting their lives on the line, and getting victims of sex crimes the resources they need? How many pastors actually do the *real* work anymore? I just see them in the pulpits, reaping the benefits of a church salary, driving expensive sports cars, and living in their lavish homes."

"I hear you, Pastor. I definitely hear you," the long-time friend of Jhalil's commented. "I meant to ask, have you told Lorraina about this?"

"Not yet. I'm actually afraid to."

"You? Afraid?" he chuckled.

"It's a couple different aspects. She could end up really jealous, or she could be very turned off by this mission. I mean, it's a lot to take in. Her man is posing as a pimp, for lack of better words. It's something I've always been passionate about but I've never had the courage to tell any of the women I was working with. Even when I was on the streets and didn't have a title in the church, I would do this on the weekends. Whether one life was saved or fifty lives were saved, it didn't matter to me."

"That's awesome, bro. I'm proud of you. But what I'll say about Lorraina is if she truly loves and cares for you like I believe, then she will be open to helping you in this mission. She will support you as well. All you have to do is just sit down and lay everything out on the table. You need to do this especially since you're trying to marry her."

"Yeah, you're absolutely right," Jhalil agreed. "I'll go for it tonight."

As Jhalil decided that the two women were lost causes and loaded up his belongings into the car, a twinge of regret and fear entered his heart. There was no telling how Lorraina would take this news, but if he knew her, then he knew she would be understanding and may even want to participate. So often, she would go around and minister to other young ladies about her promiscuous past, so surely, this would not be any different right?

He remembered a time where he was first introduced to this world—he was only a teenager. It had hurt his heart when he understood just what was taking place but he vowed from that moment on that he would dedicate his time and life to rescuing women and children in those situations.

"Sweetheart, your total is three fifty six. You are so handsome, by the way."

Jhalil smiled at the middle-aged cashier politely and reached into his back pocket for his wallet. "Thank you, ma'am."

As he pulled out a five-dollar bill, he heard a commotion in the aisle next to the checkout area, and jumped in shock. The cashier yelled out with surprise and then peeked around the cash register to see what was taking place. Items from most of the shelves flew to the floor, grunts could be heard, and the sounds of a woman whimpering were evident.

"What in the world?" he spoke to himself, but his attention was on the unusual noise.

A piece of him knew what was already going on; a woman was being beaten by her lover in the most inappropriate place. He wanted to help. However, the other part of him knew he didn't have any backup or weapon on him should anything get too crazy. Still, the gentleman in him was concerned.

As he paid the cashier and told her to keep the change, he snatched his plastic bag from the counter and rounded the aisle.

"Hey!" he called out.

Sure enough, there was a surprisingly scrawny man bent over with his pants half hanging down. The man wore boots that slammed into a girl, no older than Jhalil. She was coughing up blood *and crying silent tears, but as her eyes opened, they landed on Jhalil. She seemed to whisper "help me" even in the midst of her moans.*

Jhalil prayed that everything ended well and went for it. He would be less of a man if he didn't do anything to stop this coward. With all of his might, he lunged for the man's waist and brought him down on the floor with him. Jhalil subdued the man's erratic motions by putting all of his weight on the guy's ribcage, and then looking over a shoulder.

The young girl was now foaming at the mouth and bleeding uncontrollably. Her body shook like a maraca. His heart dropped as he cried out, "Somebody call the police!"

The cashier ran to find help, while Jhalil continued to restrain the guy. More than thirty minutes later, he was sitting in the waiting room of the hospital where the teenager had been taken for her injuries. She was recovering well, but he wanted to wait to actually see her face before he could breathe again.

A nurse peeked from beyond the curtains of the room, and motioned him over. "Kin of Rita Canales?"

"Friend," he corrected solemnly. "How's she doing?"

"As well as expected. You may visit her for a few minutes before the doctor does his final checkup."

Jhalil escaped his daydream and remembered how he got to know her in just under fifteen minutes. He reprimanded her initially for dating someone so much older and classless, but it turned out, she had been separated from her recently deported family and had been his moneymaker for the last several years. He used and abused her body for his own twisted pleasure, and then sold it to other sick men who were willing to lay down with a seventeen-year-old.

For years, they remained good friends, up until her death. She had full-blown AIDS from a lifestyle that she had not even asked for. It disgusted him that grown men actually participated in such nonsense. It sickened him that Rita was just one of hundreds of thousands of women who had no choice but to succumb to the woes of sex trafficking. That was where his mission began.

Jhalil finally mustered up the courage in his car after a quick prayer and then decided to talk to Lorraina. But to his dismay, when he rounded the corner of the bedroom, she was gone. Every single one of her belongings was missing. Perplexed, he raced around the room to find anything; any traces of a note or sign that she was coming back. He stumbled upon a hand-written note that read:

I know EVERYTHING. Goodbye, Jhalil.

He dropped to his knees in a heap of tears. The paper flowed down to the ground like a feather and joined him on the floor. The very thing he did not want to happen had occurred, and he only had himself to blame. There was no way she knew what was really going on, because if she had, she would not have left him like this. When Lorraina fled, she had taken a part of his heart too because as he wept with confusion, his heart broke more and more.

***

Meanwhile across town…

"Noah, stay over here, honey."

Lorraina sat cross-legged in the middle of a park she had randomly passed on her way to the grocery store. The bench was rickety, the wind nipped at her ankles, and her hair blew out of control, but she felt free. For the first time in weeks, she was content and not worried about her next move. All of the foolishness surrounding Jhalil and his ungodly deeds had her stressed once upon a time, but she felt happy now to have left him.

Noah played happily in the sandbox, and she knew she would probably regret allowing him to submerge himself. She was sure cleaning him up would be a task in itself. But she would give him the world if it meant seeing that big ole smile on his face. Her future as his mother was shaky; she did not know what Jhalil would do once he sought revenge. So all she could do now was to enjoy moments like this.

"It's like I'm baptized in your seduction."

Lorraina's eyebrows furrowed as she continued staring ahead. The baritone was familiar and caused her insides to quiver but not in a good way. She knew exactly whom it was before turning around. It was someone she did not have the strength to face not now and not ever. It was a constant face from her past, and one she wanted to keep there. Capri.

"What did you say to me?"

"You're still so daggone fine. Dang, girl! What are you, sipping from the fountain of youth or something?"

Lorraina swallowed hard, but not out of fear or anything. She was already irritated by his choice of words and the look in his eyes. She turned back around and pretended that he was not behind her. There was absolutely no way that he was still hung up on their affairs from once upon a time.

"Oh, so you're going to tune me out? I guess you were always good at that."

"Yeah, and you were always good at being CRAZY. What are you doing here?"

"It's a free, public park isn't it? Why can't I be here, enjoying the weather, like you? I literally was taking a walk and saw the back of your head. Plus, I know that body any time of day."

He settled on the opposite end of the bench where she was seated. In his hand was a cigarette that he lit up with a few flicks of the thumb. Leisurely, he sucked from the cancer stick with his full lips, and then blew a line of smoke in her face. She fanned it away and then began to gather her belongings.

"Leaving so soon? I was just about to give you a piece of my mind."

"Haven't you done that more than enough times already?"

He did not answer her. He only stared her down and then shook his head thoughtfully. "I used to LIVE for you. Most importantly, I used to love you."

She was silent as she settled back in her seat.

"I wanted to marry you once upon a time. I thought you could do or say no wrong. You were my everything, sweetheart. I don't even think you realize what kind of power you had over me," he commented and then gave his cigarette a long draw again.

"What we had was temporary, and it gave us the high we were searching for at that time. But marriage? You know we would have never worked, whether I was leading in the ministry or not."

Capri slid over on the bench. His hand cupped the back of her neck, and he caressed the side of her face with his thumb. Then his fingers dropped to her neckline, slid over the curve of her breasts, and then landed in her lap. His large hand closed around her thigh and he squeezed it suggestively. Lorraina pushed his arm away in disgust.

"Stop it!"

"You can't say you don't miss what we had."

"I *don't*. I'm a CHANGED woman," she affirmed softly.

"Yeah, okay," he chuckled and said.

He continued to speak, referring back to what she had told him earlier.

"But you're right. We would have never worked out. It took me, leaving my wife, to see what I had all along. I mean, let's face it, you were incredible in bed, and I'll never forget what you did for me, but I want my wife back. It had to have been God that led me to see you today."

"Your *wife*?"

"Of course. My wife. You heard from Kylie? I haven't seen her since the day we separated."

Lorraina paused and could feel her heart drop. "Are you...*serious*? You really don't know?"

"Know what?" Capri was obviously perplexed.

"Kylie's dead. She…she was shot and killed by police." The words still sounded weird rolling off of her tongue.

Capri's already fair complexion seemed to turn even paler as he paused with the cigarette hanging from his mouth. He studied her facial expressions and saw that she was as serious as a heart attack. Only a single tear welled up in his left eye and then spilled over onto his cheek.

"What do you mean, she's dead? When did this happen? H—how did it happen? What was she doing to make them KILL her? Why didn't anybody call me?"

Capri had a million and one questions, and Lorraina only had a few answers. She shrugged on her cardigan and called for Noah. As he turned around and headed for her, she answered Capri solemnly.

"We killed her. Our affair killed her. And truth be told, this conversation is killing my peace. Goodbye, Capri."

With that, she propped Noah on her hip, and then turned around and walked away. Capri yelled out in agony, but Lorraina faced forward to avoid growing emotional again. She had cried all of her last tears over her deceased friend. In a sense, their actions of being secret lovers had not literally killed her but it had led her to confront Lorraina irrationally with a gun, which led to her demise.

    Lorraina situated Noah in his car seat, and then headed for a place she knew would be safest; she drove and did not stop until she reached Curt's home.

    "I was hoping you came through. I got your text this morning. Are you okay?"

    He spoke lowly as he opened the door with a T-shirt and a pair of joggers on. She swallowed hard and entered cautiously. The way he leaned into the doorframe with power and authority unnerved her. Beneath his clothes, it was obvious he was one of those thick fellas; he had meat on him, but he wasn't fat. He was muscular, but not ridiculous. He was firm but a teddy bear as well.

"I'm fine…*now*."

"Did something happen?"

"No, just…just hug me."

Lorraina fell into his embrace and Curt held her as she requested. He moved them to the living room, helped her disrobe from her coat and shoes, and whispered encouraging words to her.

Curt caressed the middle of her back and then slid his hand under her shirt to unlatch her bra strap with one flick of his wrist. She protested and put out her hand.

"No. Please don't," she spoke softly.

"Shhh. You're so tense. Let me take your mind away from what he did," he declared while his hands ran over her shoulders and he attempted to massage her.

She shook her head again. "No, really. I'm fine, Curt. I just need a shower and *sleep*."

He held his hands up. "I'm not going to force you to do anything. But it's obvious you're hurting right now, and can't focus on anything but Jhalil. You keep thinking about his actions and hoping that you're dreaming. But each day that you wake, you realize this is serious, and he really did betray you. You also realize that you wasted your time and love on yet another fool—and that eats you up inside. But what do I know?" he questioned nonchalantly.

    Clearly he was enjoying making her uncomfortable. His words struck her heartstrings harshly. He was absolutely right. She hated to admit it, but Jhalil was consuming her every thought as of late. Even in her sleep, she was being disturbed with images of his smile and memories of his precious hugs and love. How could this be? She was still in shock from the first day that his secrets had come out.

    Tears sprang to her eyes like a faucet; she would not dare let Curt see her so vulnerable and broken. On the other hand, she felt safe. Perhaps he cared a lot for her because he soon offered his arms to her. She hugged him and nestled her face in the crook of his neck. His hands did not hesitate in resting along the small of her back.

"It's just so unfair," she wept.

"I know, sweetheart. It seems like the world hands its toughest battles to the most good-hearted people. You didn't deserve any of it," Curt pointed out. "I mean, seriously. If I had a woman like you, I would never leave home."

"Stop it," she snickered. "I'm sorry for wetting up your clothes."

"Don't apologize, and I was totally serious. Why would I need to look somewhere else for something I already have? You're beautiful inside and out, and it's a shame Jhalil could not see that."

"Thank you, Cu—..." As she thanked him, he covered her mouth with his.

But unlike any other time, Lorraina did not push him away. Lorraina felt some type of way. It was like she was drawn back into her old ways. She could feel her body cry out and take over her senses and inhibitions. Her broken heart and her mixed feelings caused her to end up naked and in the arms of Curt. He kissed her passionately while she protested not as much as she should have.

She knew God was looking down from the Heavens with disappointment, just as her heart cried out in frustration. There was no way she should have fallen for Curt's sweet nothings and kind gestures; how in the world did she end up giving her body to him again? God, forgive her, but it eased all of her stress.

Chapter Six

"You should probably go home so that things aren't suspicious, you know?" Curt asked her.

She shook her head in disagreement and stayed facing the wall of his bedroom. She was wrapped tightly in his sheets and both hands were tucked under her cheek. Guilt, anger, confusion, and sorrow filled her heart, and were reflected on her expression. She hated that she had been so weak just now. Curt, on the other hand, was beside her and lighting up a cigarette in satisfaction. Their lovemaking was probably a dream come true for him.

"What's the matter?" he questioned when he did not hear from her.

"Nothing. I can't go back. I don't want to live with him, knowing he's out doing all kind of foolishness," she said and eventually pulled each leg one by one out of the bed. "Thank you, though."

"For?"

"For taking my mind off of things for a little bit," she explained, as she got dressed.

"Where are you heading?" he called out to her and continued to suck on his cancer stick.

"Anywhere but home. I don't even know."

"Stay here then," he suggested and left the warmth of his bed. He approached her with his arms open. She accepted his hug. "It's no problem at all. You know I enjoy your company anyway."

"I don't know."

"Think about it," he said simply and kissed her. "I won't pressure you."

Clearly, he had a hold on her because even as she wished to leave, there was something that always kept Lorraina coming back. Perhaps it was the protection that he offered, or the companionship that she longed as she tried to figure out what life would be without Jhalil. It could also have been the sex that was amazing, but still not as good as Jhalil's. She missed him, but she refused to return home. She promised herself that she would ignore all phone calls and text messages from Jhalil.

"I'm only going back there to get my things. I left a box with some personal items in it," she told him and headed for the shower.

"Let me know if you need me." He retreated back to the bed and she could hear his snores not long after.

As she showered and then dressed in the outfit from the day before, she could feel the guilt seeping into her heart. Despite all that was going on, she had cheated on Jhalil, plain and simple. Not only that, but she knew she was grieving the Holy Spirit because she had completely broken her vow to remain celibate until marriage. She had gone back to her old ways of fornicating, and it wasn't a good look. She had allowed her emotions to get the best of her.

She decided not to disturb Curt. It would make things worse if he trailed along, so she went back to Jhalil's house to grab her garments and everyday necessities. Thankfully, his car wasn't in the driveway, so she had time to herself. Hurriedly, she walked through the house and stuffed her few remaining items into a duffle bag she brought along. As she picked up the last of her makeup and personal hygiene items, she could hear a car door slam in the distance.

Her heart dropped. It could either be a neighbor, or it could be Jhalil. With her luck, she was certain it was her ex. Sure enough, as she looked out the bedroom window, she saw him exiting the car and admiring her car that was positioned in his spot. If she could, she would have slapped herself for taking so long. It had been exactly twenty-two minutes that she had been scavenging through the house. Now she would have to face him.

She swallowed the lump in her throat and prepared for the worse as she headed downstairs. By now, he was entering the house and calling her name. "Where are you, love?"

Just the sound of his voice made her cringe.

"Don't call me that. Don't try to stop me. As a matter of fact, don't say *anything* to me," she warned as she approached him.

"Why are you doing this? Your note said you knew everything," he explained and tried to reach out to touch her. "What exactly do you know? I'm sure it's far from the truth."

"What did I say? Don't say anything to me. I have moved on, Jhalil, and you can call *this* off." She pulled off the engagement ring that he had given her. It had not even made an indentation on her finger—that's how quickly it was on and off.

"Lorraina, please, let me explain."

"That's the problem. You should have said something a long time ago. Maybe I would have taken you back had I known something. It's too late now. Please get some help," she suggested and shrugged off his hands. She hoisted her bag onto her shoulder and left out with his painful pleas ringing in her ears.

As she pulled off, she saw him in the doorway with his hands on his head in distress. Tears streamed down his face and she tried her best to ignore it in the rearview.

***

Weeks later, Lorraina was still at Curt's home, living rent-free and carefree. She was just arriving home from a grocery trip, and the first thing that met her at the door was Curt holding up a wrapped box. He took her brown, paper bags from her and sat the box in her unexpected hands.

"Open up," he ordered and began to put the frozen foods in the freezer.

"A gift for me?" she asked with a smile.

Life was still strange for Lorraina. She had quickly fallen into the role of Curt's *unofficial* live-in girlfriend and he loved it. She cooked, cleaned, and kept up the house like any good woman would, and he was glad that she had been broken down so easily. He thought that she would be uncomfortable with the entire idea of living together, and starting over with him. He gave her an allowance to do what she needed to do, as his thanks to her. The gifts were plentiful, and they had made love at least three more times. She felt guilty for her sins, but she had nowhere to turn to, and needed the hole in her heart filled. Curt was the perfect person.

Lorraina's petite fingers tore at the wrapping paper until a white, rectangular box was revealed. She continued to smirk as she discarded the top of the box, pushed aside the glittery red tissue paper, and then was met with a folded garment. She eased the material out of the box and held it up to her body. It was a dress that was straight out of an expensive catalogue, and was made with the gentlest of care. She could see herself in it, and she longed to fell the soft satin against her body. She wondered why Curt had gotten it for her. Not that she was ungrateful; she was just curious.

Before she could ask, he pulled her body against his so they could peer into the full-length mirror together. He held her hips in place and began to kiss along her neck as she continued to admire the dress against her body.

"You like it?" he questioned in between kisses.

"I love it. What's the occasion?"

"A work gathering. My boss is retiring after fifty-two years of service. I want you to be my date tonight."

"Tonight? Oh, wow," she whispered and slowly placed the dress back into the box.

He noticed her uninterested response and change in attitude. "What's wrong?"

"I don't know, Curt."

"What do you mean? You don't want to go with me?"

"Maybe we should slow this down—whatever it is that we have. I don't think I should go for the simple fact that we're not a couple. We're not together," she explained harshly.

"So what do you call this?" He motioned around the room and gave her an incredulous look. "Your clothes and personal items are everywhere at *my* house. You're cooking and cleaning at *my* house. We're sexing on every inch of the room, and you're saying we're not together? Oh, okay. I'm not sure what world YOU live in, but that means something to me."

"Curt..."

"You know what? Whatever, Lorraina. I'm glad I kept the receipt. I'll take the dress back and go by myself." He huffed and snatched the box from her hands.

She stared at his muscular back in shock. "So that's what you want to do? You want to storm off like you're crazy? And you think I want to be in a relationship with someone like *that*? What happened to talking things out?"

"I'm tired of talking things out! I just want to be with you. You're so stubborn that you can't see that."

"We're living in sin, and I am a former pastor. Just last month, I was with another man. That doesn't even sound right. I'm all screwed up right now, and my life has changed forever with the information you gave me, so don't fault me if I just want to take things slow. I can't afford to go through any more surprises, setbacks, or heartbreaks. I would hope that you could understand that."

"But an office party? You act like I asked you to marry me!" he yelled and then caught himself. He exhaled and calmed down some. "It's just an innocent function. I'm not asking for anything but my friend to come with me and enjoy dinner, dancing, and socializing with a bunch of old, white people," he joked.

Lorraina laughed as well and then reluctantly took his face in her hands. She did not kiss him, but she pressed her lips to his and spoke against them, "I would love to escort you to the party…*friend*."

They ate a light lunch, and then showered in separate bathrooms to prepare for the night. Lorraina was a natural beauty and her gorgeous features did not necessarily need any enhancement, but she still loved a little mascara, eyeliner, and bold lip color. She wore her dark hair down and it seemed to flow with ease since it was freshly washed. She wore a diamond choker, and a pair of diamond teardrop earrings.   The ocean blue dress was zipped up her petite back and it touched mid-thigh on her. With every stride, her toned legs could be seen. She chose shoes that had a chunky heel and showed off her shimmery nail polish. Curt mentioned dancing and she did not want to tire her feet out.

As she rounded the corner, Curt stood in the middle of the floor, buttoning his shirt. He paused and eyed her from her toes to the top of her head in awe. "You look amazing," he complimented.

"Thank you," she said with a blush. "It's a perfect fit. How did you know my size?"

"I've studied your body every time it stood before me naked. I know you have beautiful wide hips, and plump thighs. I also know you have larger breasts, and a perfectly round butt. When I saw the dress, it just called out to me; I knew it would frame your body in all the right places," he spoke passionately and shrugged as if it were no big deal.

For a second time, she blushed and remained quiet. Although she did not love him, she knew it was a reason that she stuck around. He was a charmer and he knew how to treat and talk to a woman. It would be fun seeing where this road took them, but for the time being, she appreciated his kindness and compliments.

Contrary to what Curt had told her, the room was filled with middle-aged men and women dressed skimpily. It was a diverse crowd of blacks, whites, and everyone in between. When they entered the hall, most of the individuals were kissing, hugging intimately, or just flat-out having sex. Lorraina paused as she walked in and looked at him.

"What did we just walk into?"

"I told you. It's my lieutenant's retirement party. I guess he wanted to go out with a…*bang*," Curt joked as he pointed to an older gentleman in the corner of the room who had two women on either side of him as he was fed grapes.

Lorraina must have stepped in the Twilight Zone, or some horrible nineties music video. There was no way she was going to stick around to see what happened next at this giant orgy. She felt uncomfortable and the room had an unpleasant scent already. She shook her head and turned towards the door.

"I don't want to be here."

"Oh, come on. We can just stay a half-hour and then be on our way. You're here with me. I won't let anybody do anything to you," he promised.

Lorraina still looked unsure but she followed behind him and tried to make herself feel more comfortable. They settled at an empty sweetheart table and there was a bottle of wine waiting for them.

"No, thank you," she said before he could reach for the corkscrew. "I don't drink."

"But you do everything else under the sun? Oh, okay," Curt said with a laugh. He poured himself a glass and downed it. "You sure you don't want any?"

"I'm positive." Lorraina looked around and was still in shock at what was going on around them. She felt out of place and…overdressed. She joked, "Is this what you guys normally do at the office?"

"It's a party 'round here everyday." He chuckled mischievously.

"Y'all are some kinky folks," she mumbled half-heartedly.

Lorraina and Curt were the talk of the town. Everybody's eyes seemed to migrate towards them, and then finally, a woman walked up to them as they finished their finger foods.

"Oh, my goodness. You must be Lorraina. Curt talks about you often."

"He *does*?"

"Yes, even though I knew about you before he even mentioned your name. You're that pastor who had that sex scandal going on. I watched your video that went viral. You're impressive…just stunning." She was referring to the sex tape that had been leaked by the conniving deacon at her old church.

Lorraina shuddered and realized right then that she could never truly run from her past. The woman looked at her with lust in her eyes and no inch of Lorraina's body went unnoticed. She squirmed with discomfort and looked to Curt for help, but he seemed to be enjoying this. What kind of place was this? Was this woman hitting on her? Lorraina had to get out of there.

"I think it's time to go. I'm tired, and it's been more than thirty minutes," she reminded him as she gathered her purse and began to stand.

"Leaving so soon?" the woman questioned and walked up closer to Lorraina. Her hand landed on her hip. "I haven't really gotten a chance to know you yet."

"And honey, with breath that bad, you never will. Excuse me. *Move* back," Lorraina ordered and pushed past the woman.

She could swear that she heard the woman call her out of her name, but she did not care. She had made a mistake even coming here. She had made a mistake trusting Curt to do the right thing. Obviously, his mind and intentions were somewhere else.

"Let's go now, Curt," she commanded.

She walked briskly towards the exit, but Curt was much quicker and stronger as he yanked her into his body. He whispered menacingly, "Did you have to be so rude? That was one of my long-time partners."

"Okay, and? You said you would protect me from these heathens. That woman was flirting with me. She crossed the line first."

"It's harmless. Calm down."

"I want to go home!"

He wrapped his hand tighter around her arm and then turned her to face him. "Close your eyes."

"Take me home," she demanded. "I'm serious, Curt. This is not my crowd. I don't know why you even brought me here. This isn't really a retirement party is it?"

"Close…your…eyes," he repeated and gave her a stern look. He never answered her question either.

She looked around and saw that people were staring. She reluctantly did as told and breathed out a sigh. Curt placed his hand on each side of her face, and then kissed her passionately. She could feel his tongue intertwine with hers. She also felt something grainy and flavorless that was transferred from his mouth to hers. She opened her eyes and attempted to protest, not knowing what he had done, but he held her in place.

"Stop," she mumbled against his lips and struggled to free herself. "What is that?"

Curt would not ease up. Finally, when she could sense that the tasteless mint or whatever candy that was in her mouth had dissolved, Curt released his hold on her. She slapped him with all of her strength and backed away from him. He looked shocked that she had hit him and charged towards her. He grabbed her arm so tightly that she was certain there would be a bruise there later.

"Why would you do that?" he questioned her.

"Why would you do *that*? You know what? This was all a mistake. Take me home!" she cried out and wiped her mouth. She could her mouth producing extra saliva suddenly. "What was that in your mouth?"

All eyes were on them while he practically drug her to sit down. "Lower your voice!"

"Take me home!" she screamed. "Or I'll call a cab. Either way, I'm done with you."

"Weren't you always done with me? You were always stuck on stupid and stuck on Jhalil. But I told you I get the last laugh," he warned and waved his hand to a group of men who had been watching them all night. "You gon' wish you never played with me."

Lorraina did not understand a word he was saying. She swallowed hard as she watched the men, one by one, toss a few bills on the table for the waitstaff and then made their way over. An uneasy feeling formed at the pit of her stomach. Curt was nothing but trouble and this night was confirming it more and more for her. She began to silently pray.

"Curt, my man. What's going on?" The front man of the group spoke and then nodded towards Lorraina. "Good evening, beautiful. Glad you could join us; Curt has told us so much about you."

That seemed to be the reoccurring theme. To be so new, their "relationship" sure was on everybody's minds. Lorraina kept quiet. She had no words. Besides, she was beginning to feel a little dizzy and disoriented. She could not understand what was causing her sudden illness, because she had only eaten chicken wings, cheese cubes, and a few celery sticks. She placed her hand on her stomach and nodded to the man's words.

"You're just as gorgeous as he described," another man chimed in and rubbed the hair along his jawline. "Are you ready to entertain us?"

Lorraina's eyes squinted and she cocked her head to the side. Her equilibrium was all off at this point. "Entertain *who*? Me?"

"Isn't that why you brought her?" He looked over to Curt who nodded.

Lorraina felt nauseous but managed to keep it down as she put her hands up. Her eyes were watering and she could feel her stomach rumbling with queasiness. "I'm not doing anything for anybody. I'm ready to go home…NOW!"

"Give me a second, y'all," Curt said while he reached for his phone. He checked the battery, saw that it was still pretty high, and then tossed it to one of the men. "Hook it up and play some music she can dance to."

"Who's dancing?" Lorraina asked lowly. "I'm not…I'm not d…" Her mouth felt flimsy, as if she could not form any words.

Curt chuckled and pulled her onto his lap. He kissed along the side of her face as she began to heave. "You good, baby?"

"I—I don't feel so well," she moaned. "Pl—please take me home."

"I will. Just give us one dance."

"Noooo," she whimpered and attempted to hold her head up, but it kept falling limp back onto Curt's shoulder.

He stood up and brought her along with him to the center of the room. By now, the dance floor had been cleared, and all eyes were on them as some people cheered and other people whipped out their cameras. Lorraina, unable to really verbalize any words anymore, was unsure what was taking place as she stumbled behind Curt.

"Ladies and gentleman," Curt announced in a microphone. "It would be my pleasure to introduce you to my beautiful friend, Lorraina. I wanted nothing more than to be her man, but she's rejected me time and time again."

The crowd "awwwed."

"No worries. She told me she would make it up to me now by giving you all a little entertainment. There's nothing crazier than a swingers' party, am I right?"

The people hooted and hollered in agreement.

Swingers' party? Lorraina thought. *He said it was his boss's retirement party.*

Even in her state, she realized that Curt had lied to her and brought her out here to make a fool of her. She began to drag her heavy feet off of the dance floor; it felt like each leg weighed a ton. Curt caught her as she tried to run but stumbled.

"Ah, ah, ah. Where you going? *Dance*. Otherwise I'm going to take you in the back and let Roman and Ishmael do whatever they want to you."

She followed his eyes to where two men were off to the side, staring at her hungrily. Lorraina was stuck in a room full of impure, promiscuous people that had not a moral or care in the world. She looked around helplessly as music began to play and she was ordered to dance. She felt dirty and unclean, and ignored the looks of men and women from all over as they stared holes through her clothing. She lost her balance as Curt proceeded to rip her dress apart and do everything he promised not to. She finally blacked out when several men surrounded her and led her to the back of the building.

Chapter Seven

"How does that feel, love?"

The question came as Lorraina's calves were being massaged, and she could honestly say that she needed it. She could not remember ever feeling so relaxed and tended to. The room was dark with a single candle lit, and her body was stretched across some smooth surface. She had no idea how she ended up clothed in a robe and fuzzy socks, but she could not care. The warm hands caressing her legs made it all better.

"It feels good," she whispered back.

"You've been so stressed. I wanted to ease your mind."

That voice. She quivered at the sound of that voice.

"I was thinking we should talk," he continued.

The more he spoke, the less she realized it was not Curt.

"Talk about what?" she asked while she turned to look over her shoulder.

"Let's talk about these lies they're putting on my name."

Lorraina turned completely and to her surprise, Jhalil was facing her with tears rolling down his face. She pushed away from him in disgust, but he was much too strong. He held her legs in place while he pleaded for her to stop running from him.

"Get off of me! You're SICK!" she screamed and scrambled to regain her footing, but Jhalil continued to hold her down.

"Listen to me! Everything he's told you is a lie! He's just trying to separate us."

"WHO?"

"You KNOW who! Just think about it! Please believe me!" Jhalil pleaded again.

She searched the depths of his eyes to see if he was serious. There was nothing but truth permeating his brown eyes. She reached out to cup *her hands around his face, but in an instant he was gone.*

Lorraina jumped awake in a cold sweat.

"Jhalil? Come back!" she cried out and then slapped a hand over her mouth.

Her shoulders shook in fear and her gown and hair was drenched with sweat. She felt like she had been in a sauna. Her heart thumped erratically in her chest as she tried to interpret her previous dream. All she wanted was to talk to Jhalil now. Perhaps they had all been wrong about him.

"Jesus! What is wrong with me?" she asked aloud.

Tears flowed from her saddened eyes as she looked around in the dark room and tried to comprehend where she was. Then it hit her. For the last week, she had been cooped up in the hospital. That night of the party, she had been drugged and according to the nurses assigned to her room, she had been manhandled, violated, and all but raped. The sexual assault, which had been orchestrated by Curt, was broadcasted on Facebook Live, and had gone viral up until the video was reported and taken down. For the second time, Lorraina's body had been put out on the Internet for all to see. For the second time, Lorraina's integrity, reputation, and self-esteem had been torn down and degraded. Family, friends, and old cohorts all reached out to her at the hospital to see if she was okay, including her former bishop.

    For two entire days, she had been in a coma because of the effects of the roofies that Curt had slipped in her drink and in her mouth that night. Doctors told her that it was a wonder she had survived the doses—it had to be God. But sadly, because of the ordeal, Noah had since then been handed over to local authorities to find him a forever home. It was not what she wanted, but it was court orders and she had no say so in the matter.

    It was obvious Curt really cared about her before that night's incident. The only problem was his care was obsessive and she learned that when he loved, he loved hard. He had become obsessed with loving her and loving *on* her. She realized that he was sick; he had a problem with rejection and he was still punishing her for things he could not control. He wanted to get her back for when he and Jhalil fought. He told her often that she would get the last laugh, and she assumed this is what he was talking about. He had played a game and she was his pawn—he got what he wanted. Lorraina was stripped of everything, and had to face the consequences of playing with his heart. She could hang up the idea of rebuilding her reputation; it seemed she would be known as "the promiscuous pastor" for as long as she lived.

    During this downtime, she thought of Jhalil heavily. She thought about what Curt had revealed to her, and wondered if he ever told the truth. She wondered if he had made up everything just to separate them and keep them apart. Whatever the case, she missed Jhalil dearly and could not stop thinking about his love and the beautiful history that they built. Her strange dream grabbed her attention as well; she was so confused and needed answers.

"God, wherever he is right now, please give him peace and may the truth set *him* free," she said, ending her prayer for Jhalil.

She searched for her phone throughout the mangled blankets, and then finally found the Android device. She text a message after much hesitation and knew he would not respond to her, especially with her up and leaving him. He was probably snoring up under another woman and she could not be mad at him. She didn't want his life to stop because of her foolishness. Regardless, she just needed to hear from *him*.

Her heartstrings were being pulled because she had not given him a chance. She had not allowed him to explain anything to her. Instead, she had run with Curt's words and never looked back. That was unfair and she regretted it. Hopefully, God would give them an opportunity to talk things out.

As she rolled over and got into a more comfortable position, her phone buzzed. It was Jhalil, writing her back. Correction: he was calling her back. She sighed with anticipation, looked towards the door that was still closed, and then answered the phone.

"Yes?"

"Baby! Oh, my God! What happened to you? Where did you go? Why did you leave?"

"Jhalil, we need to talk."

"Obviously! What made you run off? Just answer me that."

Lorraina closed her eyes. "Curt, and before you say anything. Tell me. Is it true?"

"Is what true?" he repeated and when she was reluctant to answer, he questioned her again. "Is what true, Rain?"

"Have you been participating in the exploitation of women and children?"

"What? Are you for real right now?" His voice grew loud and shaky with bewilderment. "God, NO! What would make you say that? Of course I haven't."

Lorraina's eyes closed. "Who were those women then, Jay? Why do you have so many identification cards and aliases? They said you had a briefcase of money. Huh? I—I even saw you out that one day with another woman having dinner. Who were they, and why were you with them? Answer me!"

"Wait. Slow down! That's why we need to talk. Of all things, why would you think I could be that lowdown and dirty? That's a coward's move! You know I could never abuse or hurt anybody, especially women or children. Those women were prostitutes that…"

"Oh, so you're admitting that you were cheating though?" she interrupted.

"LISTEN, Lorraina. You have to listen to me. You said you want the truth, and I should have given it to you long ago. I was going to pay those ladies in order to get them off the streets."

"Oh yeah?" She rolled her eyes.

"I swear to you! It's the same thing with that young lady at the restaurant downtown. Saving women from sex trafficking has been a mission of mine for a while now. I see these cats out here plotting and trying to blindside these women, and

I've tried to be an advocate for those victims for some years now. I just never knew how to come out and tell you," he explained. "You're the woman I want to marry. It was a secret that was eating me alive, but I didn't want to hurt you in any way, and look. I still ended up hurting you. Baby, you have to believe me!"

"Oh, my God," she spoke softly with remorse. "Oh, my God. I believe you. I should have always believed you. What did I do?"

"Shhh. I know it's weird and it's almost a strange thing to commit to, but God led me to complete this assignment—myself and another good friend of mine—and to date, we've helped more than thirty-two women and children."

Her heart broke all over again. This man was doing the Lord's work, while she had been over some other man's house and plotting on his downfall. She felt awful as she rubbed her hand over her forehead and tried to calm her racing heart.

"Where are you?" he pondered. "Can I see you now? I'll pick you up."

"Yes," she answered without reluctance and then looked down at her hospital garments and the IV sticking in her arm. "Wait, *no*."

"Well, where are you? Is Noah nearby you? I've missed you both so much. God, I wish I could've gotten this all squared away before this happened."

Lorraina felt two inches tall now. How was she going to explain everything that had taken place? It was like a movie that was playing out before her eyes and she was the star of it. She had to make this right no matter how she figured that this was not going to end well for her. No matter how much she planned and prayed, God Himself was going to have to step in and work everything out for her.

"Give me a day or two to come back. I promise I will. I just need…"

"Time?" He completed her sentence. "I understand, baby. Take whatever time you need. I know it's late, and I know it's still new for you. But please come back to me. I haven't been able to eat, sleep, or minister properly without you."

"I promise."

"Goodnight, baby. I'll talk to you soon, okay? I love you."

"Yeah. I—I love you too."

She nodded as if he could see her and then ended the phone call. No sooner than she tucked her phone under her pillow and begin to weep did a knock sound at her door. Of course, it was Curt who should have been locked up and away in somebody's prison. She attempted to reach for the button that would alert the nurse, but by then, he was standing before her and yanking her arm down. He went back to lock the doors and then walked to the bed.

"You're awake."

"Yeah."

"Everything all right?"

"No. Not at all," Lorraina admitted. "And you know why everything's not alright."

She decided not to reveal to Curt that she had talked with Jhalil. She wanted to play dumb for the moment. After all, he was dangerous, and he was the one who had given her the false information. His motives this entire time had been to get closer to her, and like an idiot, she had fallen for his lies. Come to think of it, she had never seen a badge, squad car, uniform, or federal agent's ID. She had not been to his workplace nor did she really believe that Curt was really who he said he was anymore. All she had done was follow her emotions, and it had gotten her in deep trouble. She had been fooled and then assaulted by strangers, and had nearly lost the love of her life in the process. None of this had been worth it.

"What's the matter?" He saw the look on her face and furrowed his eyebrows.

Her innocent act could not be contained any longer as she spoke out angrily, "You need to leave immediately. Are you kidding me? Why are you here like everything's okay?"

"What do you mean?" Curt sat on the edge of the bed and rubbed her leg. "Would you like a foot massage?"

"Don't touch me! You're a liar, and you put me in harm's way!" she yelled and attempted to reach for her cell phone on the food tray. "Curt, how long have you been a federal agent? Where's your office located?"

He cocked his head. "What's with all of this? I told you what I did for a living."

"No, Emilio and Julio did. I have no idea who they are or who they're working for. What was the purpose of lying on Jhalil?"

"What are you talking about?" He kept an unreadable expression on his face. "Are you serious right now? You think I lied to you?"

"I'm not saying anything. I just want to know where is your proof for all of this?"

Curt gritted his teeth. "So you still love him. Is that what it is?"

"I'll always love him," she vowed and looked him in the eye. "Now, tell me the truth."

He stood up and snatched the covers from the bed angrily. Then he took her by the arm and threw her down. She tumbled onto the floor and winced in pain while he ranted, "After all I've done for you. I've given you a place to stay. I gave you money! I've cooked MEALS for you. I've purchased necessities for YOU. This is the thanks I get? I loved you!"

"Curt, cut the act," she screamed from the floor. "You left me out there to be touched and violated by sick, perverted men! You put me out there on the Internet where people laughed at me, mocked me, and called me all kinds of names. You lied to me so that I could leave Jhalil. That's not love. You caused all of this!"

"*I* did that? Nah, you sleepin' around and playin' with people's emotions did that!"

"I didn't play with your emotions. I don't know what to think anymore about you. I tried to give you the benefit of the doubt, and all you've done is continue to harass and hurt me. Do I owe you something? Just tell me that. What do you want from me exactly?"

He knelt down beside her and looked at her with disgust. "After all that body's been through, and after all the men that have touched you, I'm a fool to think that I was worthy of it."

"Don't you dare talk down on me now that I've figured out this game you're playing. You weren't worried about how men I've been with when you were sleeping with me! Why do you hate me and Jhalil's relationship so much?"

"Because he can't love you like I can!" he yelled, and his voice seemed to shake the walls. "Just wait! You haven't seen the last of me, Lorraina. Go home to your man and enjoy him while he's still free."

Okay, he was truly delusional, but she also knew his threats might be serious. As he stormed out of the room, she yanked the IV out of her arm, and gathered her belongings. She did not even care to get fully dressed and ignored the nurse's pleas for her to take it easy.

She caught an Uber home and hoped to God that by the time she got there, Jhalil was still awake and she could explain everything to him. Time went by quickly, and before long, she sat outside of what was once their home. She banged on the front door and leaned against it. She could almost smell his cologne seconds before he opened the door. Lorraina jumped into his unexpected arms and cradled her face in his neck.

"I'm so sorry, baby! Please forgive me," she pleaded.

"Shhh. What matters now is that you're back here with me." He did not realize she had on a hospital gown; that's how emotional he was as he cradled her in his arms.

They both cried as he maneuvered their bodies away from the door and upstairs.

"What happened to us?" he asked softly. "Don't ever leave me again."

"I won't. I promise," she vowed.

He looked down at her body in curiosity. "Why do you have this on? What happened to you?

Did Curt hurt you?" There was anger in his eyes and timbre in his voice.

She almost wanted to smile because she could feel the love permeating his body. He still loved her and he cared about her well-being.

"Let's just talk in the morning," she suggested and kissed his cheek. "I need a bath and sleep. We can get everything out in the open another day."

But that conversation never happened. It was in the wee hours of the following morning that they were each jolted from peaceful slumber. Lorraina lifted her head from Jhalil's chest where they had fallen asleep on the day bed. She could hear two knocks and then a loud *bang*. Before long, voices and footsteps rushed in like an army. It was like they were in a movie scene, where police raided a drug lord's home and searched for weapons and narcotics. She held the blanket up to her body as she watched police officers storm into the room and command to know where Jhalil Harrison was.

He held up his hands, told them his name calmly, and then was tackled to the ground. Lorraina cried out as police officers arrested the man she was madly in love with. Lorraina prayed to the Heavens in panic as handcuffs were thrown on Jhalil's wrist. He was taken forcefully down to a police car where he was told his rights.

"Why am I bring arrested?" he questioned for the umpteenth time.

Finally, the only other black police officer turned to him and replied, "You're being arrested for the assault, verbal abuse, and threats that you made towards Mr. Curtis Randall. Watch your head."

Lorraina stumbled against the concrete in shock, and watched as Jhalil was ushered into the vehicle.

"Call my lawyer! Don't say anything to anyone about this. I'll be okay, baby. I'll see you soon," Jhalil promised shakily.

Even he seemed unsure of his fate.

Their eyes locked through the window and she shed a tear for him. Red, blue, and clear lights flashed but no sirens rang out into the night. Instead, the car pulled off and disappeared down the road within a few nanoseconds. A few of their neighbors rushed out to see what had taken place, but she ignored their questions and ran back into the house. The fingers could only point to one vengeful person again—*Curt*.

Chapter Eight

There was no way that this was happening. There was no way that Jhalil had just been arrested. Lorraina rushed to get dressed, and then searched his office until she came across his lawyer's name and number. She explained the situation to the attorney, tucked a wad of money in her purse, and then headed for her car so that she could go to the local precinct.

A dark car waited outside of their home now, and she knew who it was before he even left the confinements of his sports car.

"Why are you playing games?" she pondered with a scowl. "Somehow I think that's what you wanted all along."

Curt leaned against his car and crossed his arms. "I told you, I was going to have the last laugh in this, right?"

"You are crazy, you know that? I hate you!" she screamed with infuriation.

"No. *You're* the crazy one; you slept with me and then you go crawlin' back to your man? That's not a good look, Lorraina."

"Why would you trick me like that? You knew what you were doing all along and then you made Jhalil out to be this monster."

"You're right. I *did* know what I was doing. Jhalil told me all about his mission when we first met, and told me how nervous he was to tell you. I used what I already knew and played along with it to my advantage, and most importantly, I got what I wanted out the deal. *Sue* me."

Lorraina lunged for him but he dodged her arms and held her in place. The strength of his arms overpowered her, so her struggle was no match for him. He looked unbothered and unimpressed with the way that she was fighting against him.

"Are you done?" he questioned.

"How could you do this to me?"

"Get over yourself, Lorraina. You can't go around screwing people over and then the second someone does something to you, you want to act like a victim. It doesn't work like that."

Lorraina spat in his face. It was a lowdown move and she was surprised at her own boldness, but she could not help herself. Curtis jumped back in surprise and released his hold on her in the process. He shook his head in disgust and swiped a hand across his face. No sooner than when his vision was clear did he take the back of his hand and slam it into the side of her face. She fell down because of the forcefulness.

"Leave me alone!" she screamed. "Don't…don't touch me or say anything else to me!"

He mumbled a few words in frustration that she could not understand and then reached into his back pocket. He slammed a box down into her lap and turned to walk away. It was a ring box.

"To think that I was going to propose to you," he whispered.

"I don't *love* you, Curtis, nor do I want to be with you. Why can't you understand that? Jhalil has my heart. A proposal would not have changed anything."

He said nothing more and then settled in his car.

She could not understand why he would even waste his time. It was not like they were head over heels in love. They had slept around a few times, went on a few mediocre dates, and engaged in casual conversation; there was nothing more to their story. He had comforted her while she was going through, but ultimately, it was his lies that had pushed her into his arms.

Perhaps there was truly something off in his mind to make him do these things. Whatever the case was, she could not understand why she continued to find herself in the wrong situations with everyone from Capri, to Curtis, and even with Jhalil.

She remained planted on the ground even as he zoomed off down the driveway in his car. She tossed the ring somewhere in the bushes and reluctantly picked herself up off of the ground.

She had to get to the bottom of this and free her man.

Lorraina's first stop was attempting to follow the police car that had taken Jhalil away. She jumped in her car and took off down the lonesome road, searching for the police car. There was no spotting of any squad car; even as she squinted and looked far ahead, she could see no indication of a law enforcement vehicle. She was confused.

This particular road was the only one that people could take until they reached the main street so she was confused by its emptiness. Her neck careened around the area, and she caught movement out of the corner of her eye. Her first thought was a deer hiding in the bushes so she swerved and stayed close to the side of the road.

But no deer ever appeared. She rolled down her window and swallowed hard. "Who's out there?"

When she heard a slight rustling, she thought of the *Lifetime* movies where people stuck around and got murdered, so she sped off and did not look back. She headed to the only precinct that she knew of. In fact, it was the *only* precinct for miles, so she knew Jhalil had to have been booked here. She was surprised when everybody looked at her like she was crazy.

"You said your boyfriend was arrested? Ma'am, this town is as slow as a tortoise. We haven't had any arrests or disturbances since last month."

Lorraina shook her head and stared at the man who had a southern drawl. "What do you mean? You guys JUST left my house."

"Impossible. We're short staffed today, and the few who are here have been sitting around talking for the last few hours. No one has left this building and I would know…I'm the executive secretary," he said proudly.

Lorraina smiled sarcastically. "Good for you. Seriously, I need to clear my fiancé of whatever charges he may have. It was all a big misunderstanding."

"Ma'am…if it'll ease your concerns, would you like to take a look at our booking area? There is no one here."

Lorraina followed him around the building and sure enough, there was not a single criminal or regular civilian in sight. This police station was literally waiting for something—anything—to happen. Lorraina, though she was confused and growing agitated, could not help wondering how boring that must be for all of them to have nothing better to do.

"Thank you for your help," she said dejectedly and walked away.

As she headed to her car, she could hear them laughing through the open windows at her foolishness. They thought she was either on crack and hallucinating, or just carrying out a joke too long. She settled in her car and hit her hands against the steering wheel in frustration.

"What do I do? God, what do I do? Where could you be, Jay?" she asked no one in particular. This was killing her.

She suddenly got the urge to head back home so she drove a little bit above the speed limit and headed to Jhalil's house. This time, as she drove through the well-manicured trees surrounding the driveway, she slowed down and eyed the area where she had heard movement earlier. Her eyes caught a trail of blood leading further up the road, so she followed it and prayed the entire time.

There was either an animal hurt, or it was whom she feared was hurt.

"Jhalil. Oh, my God," she whispered emotionally and finally saw him crawling in the opposite direction.

She parked and rushed out of the car and called out to him. His shoulders were slumped and his head was lowered. He crawled at a slow pace and fell every so often. His knees and the palms of his hands were bloodied. His nose looked disfigured, as if it had been broken under the force of someone's fists. There was a deep cut above his eyebrow and purple and blue bruising had already claimed his once flawless skin. He breathed shallowly.

"Who did this to you?" she cried out and dropped down beside him. The question was rhetorical but he shook his head and tried to verbalize an answer. "Shhh. Save your breath. Hang on, baby."

She could just cry right then and there, but she held it together so that she could call for help. The dispatcher on the other end promised that an ambulance would be over shortly. In the meantime, she took off her windbreaker, and wrapped him tightly in it. She rocked his body back and forth and stayed on the ground with him while her headlights blared in their faces. It grew colder and rain began to fall just as she caught the faint sirens of an ambulance.

"Help is on the way, baby. Help is on the way."

Chapter Nine

Jhalil's mind raced a mile a minute as Lorraina sobbed and held him in her arms. Even with so much pain and discomfort, he could not help thinking if this was all part of some sick plan she had to make him suffer. He knew everything; Curt had run it down to him detail by detail in the short ride in the unmarked police car. He thought back to what had just taken place and could not seem to wrap his mind around any of it.

"You understand why you're in this car?"

"I ain't saying anything else until my lawyer is present," Jhalil said and continued to look out the window.

"Naw, naw. I think you misunderstood my question," another voice entered the conversation.

Jhalil's eyes widened as he looked at the hooded individual in the passenger seat that he hadn't noticed before. It was Curt and he wore a smug grin on his face. It was then that he realized his entire thing was a setup. Jhalil rolled his eyes and knew he had just entered into some mess. This man was still butt-hurt about him being with Lorraina and obviously couldn't handle rejection well.

"Long time, no see, my man," Curt spoke lowly.

"Let me out of this car. Let me out of these cuffs."

"I'll do so when I'm done," he said just as the car slowed to a stop. They had not covered much distance from the house. In fact, if Jhalil was able to turn around in the cuffs, he could still see the lights from his house in the near distance. Curt handed the driver a set of keys and then ordered, "Jerome, go pull my car up from down the street."

Jhalil eyed Curt as he exited the car and then came to his door. He opened it and Jhalil fell out slightly. He struggled to pull him up, and then finally was able to prop him up against the car.

"What is this? What kind of operation are you running?"

Curt punched him in his stomach and then shook his balled fist. "I'm the one that's going to be doing all the talking, you hear? Unless I ask you a question, keep your mouth closed."

Jhalil coughed and attempted to stand back up. The second he was able to compose himself, Curt punched him again in the same spot, and then kneed him in the groin. Jhalil fell to the ground this time and groaned. Curt chuckled.

"What's wrong? You can't take a punch?"

"Get these handcuffs off me and I'll show you what I can do," he said in between moans. "I did it before and you better hope I don't get the opportunity to lay you out again."

"Wah, wah, wah," Curt mocked and kneeled down beside him. He held something in his hands. It was rectangular and black. Jhalil kept his eye on it until he was sure what it was. "Listen up. I'm going to make this short because I know your little whore will be on her way soon to find you."

Curt adjusted the object in his hand. It looked to be a recording device of some sort, because with a few presses of the red buttons, he could hear Lorraina and Curt's voices. It was clear as day that they were breathy and in close proximity of one another. There was also the sound of lips touching skin, occasional moans, and the delicate thump of a headboard slamming against a wall. Finally, Lorraina cried out on the recording and told him that she had had enough, and the creak of mattress springs could be heard as the recording faded.

Jhalil wished he could block out the audio, but it was impossible. Curt held him down with his knee in his side, and began to play another portion of the recording.

"You promise to protect me?" Lorraina asked.

"I'll do anything you want me to do."

"What if Jhalil comes back and wants revenge? I'll help you take him down, but I need to know I'm safe when all this is said and done."

"I got you. I'll handle him. I'll make it so he disappears if you want me to."

"No, no. Don't do that. Don't kill him. Just teach him a lesson. Someone I trusted abused me as a child so my tolerance for this is nonexistent. Pedophiles of any kind deserve to be beaten and tortured."

"You want my guys to do that to him?"

"Do whatever you want. I don't care. But don't kill him. I just want to be done with…"

The recording stopped. Jhalil's eyes widened in shock as their conversation registered in his mind. Curt kept quiet as he tucked the recorder in his pocket and then stood to his full height.

"I'm only doing what she asked," he said before slamming the heel of his foot into Jhalil's back and side.

Curt kicked him in the face, crushing his nose. He proceeded to beat him up a few more minutes, before dragging his body into the shrubbery, and then unlocking the cuffs from around his wrist. Jhalil watched helplessly as Jerome pulled up in Curt's sports car, and he hopped back into the *unmarked police car. Curt, instead of following Jerome, headed back to Jhalil's house.*

Although he was shocked by Lorraina's harsh words, he prayed to God that Curt didn't hurt her as he drifted in and out of the darkness calling him. He finally came to when he heard a car slow down near where he was slumped over.

Assuming it was Curt coming back for more, he crawled as quickly as he could on a possibly shattered tibia, and throbbing, sliced hands. Curt had cruelly run his pocketknife across each of his palms. But it wasn't Curt; it was not Jerome, or any other fake police officer returning. It was the woman he had grown to love and hate and the woman who had gotten him in all of this mess.

"Who did this to you?"

He could hear her cry out as he finally breathed out and trusted that he would no longer have to fight for his life. He was out cold.

***

"Mr. Harrison?"

Jhalil stirred awake just as he felt a set of cool hands that were wrapped in latex gloves, probe at his stomach. He winced and moaned for the woman to stop.

"I'm sorry. I just want to make sure there are no blood clots," the nurse assured him.

"What happened to me?"

His throat was thick with swelling, and his voice was hoarse. His breath smelled horrid. He eyed the young woman who was probably no older than twenty-two or twenty-three and fresh out of a college internship. She had rich, brown skin and the kinkiest, most beautiful hair he had ever seen that was flowing past her shoulders. She was petite with dimples for days and wore distinctive, purple nail polish.

"Mr. Harrison, you favor Odell Beckham Junior," she said as she began to peel away the soiled gauze that had been on his abdomen.

He winced in agony. "I've been told that before. Now can you tell me what happened to me?"

She looked unsure to speak. "Your injuries are not life threatening, thankfully. Your surgery went well for your broken rib."

"Broken rib?"

She nodded and brushed a tendril of hair out of her face. "You don't remember anything?"

"Vaguely," he groaned as he attempted to survey the damage on his body, but all he saw was the aqua-colored hospital gown and white surgical wrap.

He watched the woman pump a quarter-sized amount of sanitizer into her palms and rubbed her hands together. She headed for the door while speaking, "Don't move too much. You'll rupture your incisions and disband your stitches."

"What did I need stitches for?" Jhalil wondered and felt along his body with one of his hands.

"Your chest, eyebrow, and your leg."

"What happened to my leg?"

Slowly, the night's events came back to his remembrance. He remembered being hit in the head and feeling a sharp pain in his chest as Curt stomped it. But he couldn't recall what had happened with his leg.

"It looks like someone kicked and broke your shin in three different places. Fortunately, no main arteries were severed and doctors were able to save your leg. You'll definitely have to have therapy, Mr. Harrison, but it's touch and go if you'll be able to even use that leg again," she spoke softly and with sincerity. "I'm so, so sorry."

Jhalil's heart dropped. He could feel his eyes become watery at the thought of losing mobility in his leg. He grew emotional because there was no reason for him to be sitting here now, at the expense of the love of his life's mistakes.

"I'll give you a minute. But you do have a visitor if you're up for it. She says she's your fiancée. She drove behind the ambulance that brought you."

Jhalil shook his head and ignored the woman's words. More than anything, he could not figure out why Curt always tried so hard to take him back to the old Jhalil—the one who had no heart and who was once as ruthless as they came. He had God on his side, but God Himself would have to stop him from putting a hurting on Curt. As soon as he was up and walking again, he vowed to get his sweet, sweet revenge. As for Lorraina? He had no words for her right now. After all, she was the root of all of this mess.

"Tell her to go home and don't ever come back here."

The nurse reluctantly nodded and left out. "Oh! Okay. Right away, sir."

As the door closed behind her, he broke down crying as he tried to imagine life without the use of one leg.

Chapter Ten

"Mr. Harrison would rather not have company at this time."

"What do you mean? I'm sure he would want to see me," Lorraina protested as she stood up. "Did you tell him who I was?"

Her legs had begun to cramp up and she was tired, but she was determined to stay for as long as she could, if it meant supporting him through his recovery. Lorraina looked at the nurse who appeared uncomfortable and unsure about her request.

"I told him his fiancée was here and those were my instructions…to tell you to leave," she said with her head lowered.

She turned to walk away and Lorraina stared at the woman's back in confusion and slight anger. Who did this woman think she was? There was no way that Jhalil had given her such ridiculous orders. He was probably excited to see her and wanted a familiar face after such an eventful night. Lorraina ignored the nurse's protests, and brushed past her.

"Ma'am, you cannot go back there!" the nurse called out while the secretary paged for security. The uniformed men came quicker than expected and Lorraina soon found herself being hoisted into a pair of muscular arms and physically carried out of the hospital.

"Don't make me call the police," one of the men threatened and stood in place until Lorraina turned around and headed to her car.

She was hurt, furious, and offended—why was the staff making it so hard to check up on her man? Had Jhalil really said that after all? Lorraina could not figure it out, so she decided to call it a night; she would go home and come back tomorrow when the staff shifts changed. She cleaned up the mess of Curt's staged invasion, and buried herself under the sheets.

The next morning, she did exactly what she planned. She went to the hospital, signed in under a different name, and marched into his room. She was prepared to throw a tantrum or two if anyone said anything. But surprisingly, there was no one in sight to protest her presence. As she rounded the corner and pulled back the curtain, she was puzzled to see a woman's backside facing her. This woman was not a nurse because she did not have any scrubs on. She wore jeans that were too tight, a T-shirt that rode up her midriff, and a simple ponytail.

From the build, Lorraina already knew who it was. It was someone she never thought she would run into ever again, especially in the company of Jhalil. It was his ex, Kenya, and she looked absolutely beautiful even with her casual clothes on. Why was she here, and leaning over his bed? Why was she helping to feed him mashed potatoes, and wiping his face? Lorraina had so many questions.

"Ahem." She cleared her throat loudly.

Kenya whipped around and looked surprised to see someone else in the room. "Hi, can I help you?"

"You can help me understand why you're here with my man, doing my job?"

"Obviously, if you were on your job, he wouldn't be here in the hospital."

"Ladies…that's enough," Jhalil said weakly and attempted to sit up on his own. "Kenya, go down to the cafeteria for a second. Lorraina, come in and pull the curtain back. We need to talk."

Lorraina did as told and sat on the edge of the bed while Kenya snatched up her purse from the windowsill and walked out. Jhalil looked better than what she imagined, especially because the last time she saw him, blood was everywhere. Still, she cringed at his bruises, bandages, and stitches, and felt guiltier at Kenya's words. She was not totally responsible for Curt's actions, but she had literally slept with the enemy, so it made things just as bad.

"So, what's up, Jhalil? You're runnin' back to her now? What is this?"

Jhalil nonchalantly glanced at her and the fire in his eyes made her stop in her tracks. He stared her down coldly for several long moments, and then looked at the muted television screen.

"You have no room to talk or say anything. Thank you for calling for help that night—but that's as far as my kindness will go today."

Lorraina swallowed hard. "Baby…"

He held up his hand. "Kenya's the one who showed me that video online of you dancing and allowing those men to do those things to you. Not only that, but Curt played a recording of you two making love and talking, and you said you wanted him to hurt me? Over what? How could you do me like that? I could've died that night, and God only knows if I'll be ever to use my leg again. It's all your fault."

"Don't do that to me…don't you dare say that to me. I was tricked and assaulted!"

"So was I! The only difference is, you had a choice to stop it before it happened. You didn't have to run to Curt. You didn't have to leave me. You CHOSE to take his word over mine and got yourself in that situation. Look at you! You've changed and it's not in a good way!"

"He had EVIDENCE that you could possibly be…"

"Evidence? The man doesn't even have a badge, Lorraina! How stupid can you be? That man lied to you! He's a con artist, and he didn't take well to your rejection, so he did what he had to do and he got what he wanted. He got you in the bed *again*, and he almost killed me. He knew that if he got in your mind, he could strike me next. Now, I can't use one of my legs, and I can't go forth in my ministry. You can hang it up on marriage or even a relationship. How can I marry somebody like you? There ain't a faithful bone in your body!"

Lorraina could cry. She sat there, numb to it all. "So you're throwing our relationship away?"

"Didn't you do the same? I would have taken you back and forgiven you off the strength of knowing that you were blindsided. But you slept with him. That wasn't a mistake. You made a choice to cheat and that is what I cannot accept. Not only that, but your actions took Noah away. I loved that little boy and planned to adopt him! You should have just come to me. If you loved me, you should have fought for us and gotten to the bottom of it, instead of taking some psycho's word over mine." His voice was growing more hoarse from raising it. He sat back in his bed and sighed. He looked worn out.

    Lorraina was fully crying now. Jhalil had quickly become her life; other than God, she lived for him. She did not know what she would do without him and the thought killed her as she pleaded for him to take her back. He explained that Kenya was helping him through the remainder of his recovery, and how he wished he had never left her in the first place. He told Lorraina that she had been nothing but trouble since day one, and he should have stayed away. He ordered for her to leave and to never contact him ever again. Lorraina felt dead inside. She literally had no one, and her and her promiscuous ways had caused her own destruction.

    That night, as she popped a melatonin vitamin that would help her go to sleep, she settled in a warm bath and contemplated life. She thought about how gullible she had been when it came to men. She thought about how careless she had been when it came to her body. She even thought about her childhood and how her sex drive was first explored.

There was a man in her neighborhood—named Eugene—who all the kids loved and trusted. He was the ice cream man, and he would often give leftover treats to the children. He was in his early twenties, and to Lorraina, he was as tall as the trees in her grandmother's backyard. All the girls thought he was cute because of his smooth, cinnamon-colored skin, and deep, green eyes that would turn hazel in the fall. He seemed to take a liking to Lorraina especially; she always received two treats while the other children only received one.

It was on a really hot day in August that she finally got to tour his ice cream truck. To her surprise, he only allowed her to board the truck while her friends ran off in tears of disappointment. She was shown all of his fine equipment and then given a cherry-flavored Popsicle. As she licked its contents, she noticed how his eyes widened and how he shifted in his seat. She blushed under the gaze of his eyes and continued to suck on her treat.

"Can I show you one last thing?" he questioned her.

"Mmhmm," she mumbled with her lips still stretched around the cold treat.

Eugene unzipped his pants right then and there and both Lorraina's treat and jaw dropped at the sight of his exposed flesh. She began to cry with anxiety and headed for the door. Her Popsicle fell to the ground and splattered all over her blue jeans. Her guardians had always taught her right from wrong, and this was definitely wrong, even coming from Eugene.

"Where are you going?" he asked in panic.

"HOME! I'm tellin'!" she cried out and could not seem to shake the images of Eugene's body part. As she ignored his pleas to keep it a secret, she raced home, and the picture of his manhood stayed with her for the rest of her life.

A single tear fell down Lorraina's tear now, as she realized she had always been curious about intercourse and the opposite sex from that moment on. There was nothing she could do to stop it, cure it, or make sense of it. No prayer, no counseling, and no girl talk could truly satisfy her appetite when it came to love making. She wondered if something was wrong with her. She never admitted it to anyone, but she also had been touched a couple times on the school bus as a fifth grader; she had been touched in college by a professor, and in the workplace by a supervisor. It was like she was a magnet for assault—but why? What was so special about her?

She loved sex—*that*, she could confess. She loved the idea of creating music and magic with her body; she loved the thought that others craved what was between her legs. It was always something that gave her confidence, assurance, and validity as a woman. No matter how much women like her were looked down upon, she enjoyed the attention and the looks. But it wasn't healthy. As a woman of

God, she should have a completely different mindset, but it was hard to do when sex was all you knew.

Sadness crept into her heart. Her addiction had been costly. Even now, as her hands touched her body, she thought of Jhalil and knew his intimacy would be something she missed more than anything. She grew sick at the thought that he could no longer frequent her body.

"God, please," she whispered as she began to drift off to sleep in the bathtub. "If you do nothing else for me, I thank you. But please deliver me from my illness. Please take away my addiction."

Chapter Eleven

It was the very next week that God honored Lorraina's prayer request. She was absently watching a soap opera when a commercial took over the television screen and encouraged viewers suffering from addictions to call the listed hotline. She scribbled the number down, reached for her cell phone, and took a deep breath. She dialed the numbers shakily, and then waited.

No one answered.

She decided to leave a message for the extension. She whispered as though she was in a room full of people, but really, it was only Lorraina standing in the middle of her kitchen. That is how ashamed she felt.

"Hi, I would like to remain anonymous at the moment, but I, um…I was calling because…because I have an addiction. I am addicted to sex. It has taken control of my life. It's ruined relationships for me. It's clouded my judgment time and time again, and I'm sick of it.

Please call me back at this number when you have a moment. Thank you so much."

Lorraina ended the call and sighed. Whatever happened would happen. She could not be concerned with anything else except getting better with each day. Since Jhalil had exed her out of his life, she had not eaten like she should and the weight was just falling off of her body. Her hair had not been done in days. She had only prayed a few times, and she had completely stopped attending church.

Her life was literally in shambles and she knew God was not pleased with her.

As she prepared for bed that night, she received a call from an unknown number. Something in the pit of her stomach encouraged her to answer so she did.

"Hello?"

"Hi, my name is Doctor Rich Munn. My secretary forwarded me your number and message earlier, but I didn't get a name. I know it's late and inappropriate, but I could not help relating to your addiction. I, myself, could not live without sex or intimacy and it cost me my marriage, family, and six-figure salary. I had to reach out to you right away. Do you have time to talk more?"

"Um," Lorraina thought aloud and looked at the clock. "It is eight o'clock in the evening, however, I was only about to shower. I can talk, yes."

"What's your name, sweetheart?"

"Rain," she fibbed.

"Rain—excellent. Call me Rich." There was some rustling in the background and she assumed he was grabbing a pen and some paper. "This is my cell number, which you can keep. However, tomorrow and beyond, I'll always call you from my office, or meet with you in person. Is that doable?"

She nodded as though he could see her. "Yes, that's fine."

"Excellent," he spoke and his voice softened. "Now tell me what's on your mind? Besides dealing with your addiction, *why* did you decide that you needed professional help? Please keep in mind, this consultation and conversation is completely free."

Lorraina took a deep breath and figured it was now or never. No matter how it made her look, she would have to be honest in order to get honest results. She told him everything; she revealed most of her dealings with sexual intercourse or contact, from her childhood, to her adolescence and college years, to her adulthood. She told him about the men she had been with; she told him about the men she loved and those she only dated in order to satisfy her *craving*. She told him how she had messed up marriages and relationships, and how she was also a former pastor who encouraged others to flee from sin, but she could not even do the same. She told him about Jhalil and Curt, and their most recent falling out. She told him all of her deepest secrets.

Rich listened on the other end with a judgment-free ear, scribbled on his notepad, and suggested that they meet for dinner tomorrow night. She agreed and went to bed with a much emptier heart and conscience. The following evening, she met him outside of his office building, which was adjacent to a Chinese restaurant. She was not big on this type of food but she agreed because she needed the help.

"After you," he said politely and stepped to the side so she could enter the dim restaurant first. "Have you ever been here before?"

She sat down in the chair that he had pulled out for her. "I have not."

"They have excellent food," he pointed out and unbuttoned his suit jacket.

"Is 'excellent' your favorite word?" she joked.

"Oh, goodness. I've been told I say that too much."

"Just a little." Lorraina smiled.

They made small talk over an appetizer and just as their entrees were coming out, Lorraina noticed a couple coming in from the wheelchair-accessible ramp. She smiled compassionately, and thanked God for her legs. She turned back to Rich, who had asked her a question.

"I take that as a no?" he questioned.

"What did you say?"

"I asked if you've contacted your fiancé since your last run-in?"

"Oh." Lorraina shook her head. "No. He's probably moved on, as I should. We haven't spoken at all."

"If you never heard from him again, how would that make you feel?"

Lorraina often thought of that question and sighed. In fact, she had just sent him an 'I love you' text this morning, but of course, he had not responded. Her eyes glazed over with tears.

"It would hurt me to the core. But I have to accept the consequences of my actions. I was wrong, and my actions caused him to get hurt."

Rich nodded and looked down at his plate. "Sort of like when my wife and I split. We aren't divorced, just separated. But I realized that I was bad for her, and that I was willing to separate myself so that *she* could be free. Imagine that—a psychologist who couldn't even save his family. At the time I didn't know God, but now I do, and He's kept me since then. I miss her so much, and she won't let me see our kids, but I wouldn't want to interrupt her life again unless God tells me to go back."

"That's so real, Rich," she whispered. "I'm sorry to hear that."

"I'm man enough to accept my mistakes and consequences, as you said." He shrugged.

Lorraina bit into a piece of orange chicken and looked up when the waiter at the next table dropped a glass cup. He was standing before the man in the wheelchair and apologized. She squinted and eyed the man closer. No, it couldn't be. Of all places to be, she was in the same restaurant and breathing the same precious air as....*Jhalil*?

This was such a coincidence.

"Oh, my goodness," Lorraina said and dropped her head. "You see that guy in the wheelchair?"

"Yeah."

"That's my…" As she spoke, Rich cut off her words.

"Wait a minute. *Kenya?*" His voice was loud and overpowered the soft music playing overhead.

Kenya was accompanying Jhalil tonight and they both looked exhausted from the long week. She was helping to feed and tend to him, while he sat immobile and quiet. The two turned towards Rich and Lorraina, and Kenya's eyes got big especially.

"What are you doing here?" she asked him.

"You have no right to question me! What are you doing here, and with HIM?"

Jhalil spoke up this time and looked at Lorraina with bitterness. "You literally sent me a text six hours ago, but you're here with another man? Is this another one of your flings, Lorraina? It doesn't take you long to bounce from the next one, huh? Unbelievable."

Lorraina removed the linen napkin from her lap and stood up. "He's helping me get better! He's a psychiatrist."

Rich looked over in confusion. "How do y'all know each other?"

"That's Jhalil—the man I've been talking about to you."

"Woooow," Rich whistled and looked around. "So we all are just one big happy family right now, huh? Where are the kids, Kenya?"

"Wait, so who is Kenya to YOU?" Lorraina wondered.

"My wife," he clarified. "The one I was telling you about."

"*Estranged* wife," she corrected. "You've been runnin' your mouth to her about me?"

"It doesn't matter. We're still married, and you have no right to keep my kids from me!"

"Kids? Wife?" Jhalil repeated and looked over at Kenya with shock written on his face. "We've been on and off all this time, and you haven't told me anything about you being married with children. What the heck, Ken?"

"Let me explain!" she cried out.

Jhalil wheeled himself away, while Rich dragged Kenya outside and proceeded to scream at her. Lorraina sat back down at her seat and held her head in her hands. She had a headache forming.

Rich returned a few minutes later, seething, and trying to calm himself down. "I'm so sorry you had to be a part of that."

"It's fine."

"We can still talk if you'd like. I just don't know about that girl. I—I just don't know how I got to be so lucky with an idiot like that for a wife," he spewed sarcastically and she knew it was only the anger talking. After all, he had just professed and expressed his love to her, and now he was insulting her. "Are we done here?"

"We're done."

That was literally the last time she would ever see Rich again.

Chapter Twelve

It was now an entire month after the blowup at the restaurant, and Lorraina had not heard from Jhalil since. She knew he was on to better things, and she had no reason not to be as well. She picked up the pieces to what her life had become and asked God to put those pieces back together again. Little by little, she learned to live without him. She learned to live without a man period. She also recognized and learned self-love, and wished she could show her younger self a thing or two.

She sought after another psychologist; this doctor was a well-seasoned woman named Princess Crouch. They met three times a week in her downtown office, and sometimes outside of their sessions. They became close and she was there for Lorraina like no one ever had been. In fact, they had just left a shopping center, and were heading their separate ways. Lorraina busied herself with a part-time secretary position at Princess's office, and was now attending another church home. Life was beginning to finally look up.

After she drove back to her cozy one-bedroom, one-bath apartment, she turned on the news and was alarmed to see Curt's face all over the news. He was wanted for murder by the FBI, and he was said to be armed and on the loose. She listened to the young news anchor's report.

"We spoke to the federal agents today, and here's what they know so far," the woman announced before the screen flashed *BREAKING NEWS* across it.

The image of a detective appeared on the screen at a press conference that was held earlier. He spoke with a lisp, "Mr. Randall is charming and intelligent, but he's extremely dangerous. He not only has organized several bank robberies, but he's played a major role in the murder of twenty-nine year old, Chelsea McCullen. McCullen is his ex-wife and the mother of his six children. We have reason to believe that he is seeking revenge on any and every woman he has ever been romantically involved with, according to a letter recently found in Randall's Northside home. He is not working alone either. We have sufficient evidence that he has been working with former FBI agents, Emilio Chavez and Julio Lechuga, to commit these crimes. Randall was recently charged in the beating of local pastor and community activist, Jhalil Harrison. We are warning all civilians to be on the lookout for this dangerous, dangerous man."

  Lorraina felt sick to her stomach as she tried to comprehend what she had just heard and seen. He had truly fooled her with his gentleman act, and obviously, she wasn't the only one tricked and hurt by him. Six kids? This man had lost his mind. She felt sad about his ex-wife's death, but was also thankful to God for covering and protecting her while in the presence of Curt because he could have done anything to her. She turned off the television and immediately called Jhalil. Surprisingly, he answered on the first ring.

  "Jhalil, listen…"

He cut her off with his monotonous tone. "Yes, Lorraina. I've heard about Curt. A detective called me today and explained everything to me. Yes, this situation can't get any crazier. Yes, the thing with Kenya was a surprise and I guess it's karma for all the nasty things I said to you. Yes, I hate you and want nothing more than for you to never talk to me again."

She remained quiet, gripping her cell phone as if her life depended on it. She was relieved to hear his voice but was saddened by his harsh, unapologetic words.

He continued, "But I'm also glad you didn't end up like his ex-wife, dead, and just a memory. I would have lost my mind knowing that something happened to you and I did nothing to stop it."

She smiled in relief and felt a fresh wave of tears threatening to fall from her eyes. Unlike all the crying she had done lately, these were tears of joy.

"I know everything, Rain," he added.

"Do you forgive me?" she pondered.

"I do," he whispered back.

"Do you believe me when I say I had no idea or no say so in his attacks and plans?"

"I do believe you."

Hesitantly, she asked the number one question on her mind. "Do you still love me?"

"I love you," he spoke without reluctance. "I never stopped."

That was truly music to her ears.

"But none of it matters anymore," he said. "My life as I know it is all over."

"Why do you say that? Your life isn't over. Your life's just beginning. Don't let this define your future. God isn't done with you yet."

"I'm honestly tired of hearing all of that," he admitted and she could hear wind in the background. He must have been outside, enjoying the breeze. "I'm tired of it all. Maybe this is a dream that I haven't woken up from."

"Why are you talkin' like that? Where are you anyway?"

Jhalil sighed and there was great emotion in his response. "I just had to get away. I'm near Johnson's Pier."

"Johnson's Pier?" she repeated. "Why are you there? Who took you out there?"

"I caught an Uber. I just needed to clear my mind, you know?"

Her eyes narrowed in concern. "Be careful. That's one of the most dangerous places in the city. So many people fall in the river and drown every year," she said.

He laughed in her ear and the sound was forced and filled with agony. "Look at you. You're still lookin' out for me even after all the terrible things I've said to you."

"Who cares? We hurt EACH OTHER. None of that matters. Your happiness and peace of mind is all I care about."

"You really mean that?"

"Of course."

"I'm afraid all that's over now. Just imagine how anointed we could have been as a couple really after God," he mused quietly and sniffed. "Demons would tremble at our power…and people would be amazed at our testimonies."

"And they still can," she said.

"I'm afraid that's all over, love. I've failed God way too much."

"Don't say that! For as long as you have breath in your body, you are forgiven and can make it right! It doesn't matter what we've done or what happened in our pasts; God's grace is sufficient. You told me that same thing. Remember?"

"I do, but I can't even travel like I used to. I can't walk around freely and do what I need to do to preach the gospel. Our church has fallen apart. Our secrets are out. Who's going to join under my leadership? Not only that, but my leg is a vital part of my ministry."

"I understand that, but baby…"

"There's nothin' you can say right now. I'm sorry. This is just too much for me," he said in between a hearty cry.

"Why do you keep talking like this? What's really going on?" she questioned.

She didn't like how he sounded. She was sure that he was falling apart on the phone right then and there with her, and she feared for what may come. She headed for Johnson's Pier, which was a popular tourist spot. It was gorgeous but deadly, and had huge boulders overlooking the aggressive river. Many times people would climb on the rocks to get a good selfie in, and then would fall to their death. She hoped that was not in his plans as she headed for the door without shoes or a jacket on.

"My legs." He was openly crying now. "It turns out, not only was the right one shattered, but it's been infected since the surgery and it spread to my other leg. They may have to amputate both legs. What am I going to do without my legs, Lorraina?"

"God can do ALL things and you know that! We've got to speak healing, Jhalil!"

"I GIVE UP! You can have this life!" he yelled.

Lorraina encouraged him to stay on the line and drove as fast as she possibly could without getting a speeding ticket or getting into an accident. She prayed for his mind and for God to protect him until she arrived. She searched through the grassy lands and stumbled over wood chunks and tree stumps that had decayed. She finally saw Jhalil's silhouette as he stood on the edge of a boulder and looked down into the never-ending water. The currents were strong and brash. His crutches were tossed to the side of him. His legs were shaky and unsteady, and the only thing keeping him upright was the powerful wind that literally seemed to hold him up.

Lorraina kept her movements slow and purposeful and walked up to him with caution. She chose not to say anything until she was right behind him. Just as he dropped his phone into the water and began to fall forward, Lorraina reached out and grabbed him. Jhalil had lost quite a few pounds since his incident, but he still had a lot of weight on him, and especially his semi-paralyzed legs.

She held onto him and backed away from the edge of the boulder. He was crying and looking helpless as she pulled him to safety. She thanked God that she made it in time and hugged his body to hers.

"Baby, don't you ever leave me! You hear me? I would have died without you!" she declared.

"I'm sorry. God, I'm so sorry. I'm sorry," is all he kept repeating.

They sat there for hours, crying, hugging, praying, and rocking back and forth in the cool breeze. Eventually, Lorraina called for help and she continued to nestle against him as they waited.

"How did we get so broken?" he asked her and looked off into the distance. Tear stains coated his cheeks. "How did we each reach our breaking points like that?"

"I don't know. But only God can put us back together again," she whispered next to his ear. "This time, let's allow God to *really* heal us. I don't want to waste any more of my life on the wrong people, and on the wrong things."

He closed his eyes with a smile of agreement.

Epilogue

Five years later...

"Joshua Hardison," the dean called out over the roars of cheers and claps.

The auditorium was packed with people from wall to wall as family members, faculty, and graduates all gathered for the long-awaited commencement ceremony. Lorraina stood off to the side of the stage, knowing she was going to be called shortly, and attempted to calm down some. She was half nervous and half excited at her accomplishment. In just four years, she had completed her second Bachelor's degree in psychology, with a concentration in family therapy. God had blown her mind and taken her down a path she never expected.

Not only had she gone back to school, but she had been blessed to open up her own office building that focused on saving women, saving children, and saving families. It was filled with the best of the city's therapists and counselors, and she was thrilled to be jumping in headfirst to the role just as soon as she accepted this certificate. With her new credentials, she would be able to counsel women affected by sexual and domestic abuse, and give treatment to women who were addicted to sex. She knew her grandmother would be so proud of her.

Her eyes skimmed the crowd and she embarked on the impossible task of finding her loved ones. *Bingo*. She should have known that her husband would make some gaudy, larger-than-life sign to draw her attention. Throughout this journey, he had been so supportive and helpful when it came to the late nights of studying and preparing for her courses. Jhalil was just as excited as she was, and for that, she loved him all the more.

Upon being delivered from her sexual addiction, and thoroughly receiving the help and counseling that she needed, Lorraina accepted his proposal and it was one of the greatest decisions she ever made. They were going almost four years strong now, and were unstoppable. God had renewed their minds and ordered their steps to present one of the most effective marriage ministries to the city. They were no longer heading a church, but were elders at their church home. They had even signed with the premier publishing company called Kindred Soul, and had written a best-selling book about marriage and ministry. To date, six marriages had been saved under their leadership. Life was absolutely beautiful and Lorraina knew it was all because they accepted God's Will for their lives instead of orchestrating in the flesh.

  She waved and blew a kiss to Jhalil, and then tuned back into the older gentleman who was calling out names and awarding the graduates with handshakes. It was time.

  "Lorraina Harrison," he called out and looked at her with a smile.

  Lorraina could hear her family rooting for her, although the dean had warned everyone to keep quiet until the end. She took a deep breath and took a few steps forward in her pumps, and then raised both her index fingers. She looked to the Heavens and continued to point upward as she whispered, "It was all you, God."

She accepted her diploma, posed for a photo, and then retreated to her seat. There were close to eighty more graduates that had to be called, so she ducked low, and tiptoed out of the arena. She looked for the landmark where her husband told her to meet him. As she rounded the corner, there were balloons blowing in the breeze and a small crowd of smiling faces that greeted her. Her eyes widened in shock because she had no idea so many people were present for her special day.

"Congratulations!" everyone yelled out and she ran into the arms of her family, kissing them one by one on the cheek. She hugged Terreana, Princess, Jhalil, her pastor and First Lady, a few church members, and the people who gave her even more reason to live, her children.

There was Noah, Jhalil Junior, and Jada. After more than a year of searching, they had been reunited with Noah and were awarded full custody and guardianship of him after explaining to his family what had happened. Noah was now six, Jhalil Junior was two, and Jada was seven months. They were both seated in a stroller and looking up at their mother with bright smiles. Although she had carried them both for nine months, had a C-section with Junior, and had faithfully juggled motherhood with all of her other responsibilities, she could not believe that they both looked identical to their father.

She chuckled at the thought and looked at her husband. Jhalil was fine as ever in his baby blue button-down shirt. He had only buttoned it beginning at his navel, so his muscular, tattooed chest was showing. He wore white cargo shorts, and baby blue loafers, and had a pair of tan shades propped on top of his baldhead. Yes, her baby had completely shaved his hair off and he looked good enough to eat. The older he got, the wiser, more confident, and finer he seemed to get as well. Sexiness oozed from him even now as he licked his lips and grabbed Jada from the stroller. Jhalil noticed her watching him so he winked.

Despite what doctors said, he was still walking and running on his God-given legs. He had been completely healed and fortunately, there was no lasting damage to his limbs. She often found herself praising God for him and their journey through hell and back. He was all hers for a lifetime and beyond. She was especially thankful for being able to deliver healthy, happy babies. She would not trade her family for anything else in the world.

It was like she was a new creature in Christ all over again, but *for real* this time. She did not plan on backsliding ever again, and she would forever tell the devil to get behind her if temptation ever arose. People like Capri, Curt, and whomever else from her past were long gone. In fact, the last she heard was that Capri moved out of town to start a new life, and Curt was locked away to rot in some prison. She felt good. She felt free.

Lorraina unzipped her black graduation gown and tucked it on top of the stroller. She kept her cap on, and made sure her long tresses were still beautiful and vibrant beneath it. She wore a flowy maxi dress and opted to remain sleeveless because it was so humid out. Gold earrings and bangles completed her attire.

"Where to now, baby?" Jhalil asked and led them to the corner of the intersection. They had parked in a structure not far from the arena. He leaned over to kiss her, and then placed his hand on the small of her back.

"I'm so glad y'all could make it," she told everyone and grabbed Noah's hand as they crossed the street. "Now let's eat!"

The End

THANKY YOU FOR READING –
Other Titles From the Author

* Andrue & Symone: An Urban Love Affair 1

& 2

* What God Has Joined Together 1 & 2

* Soul Cry

* Sins of a Mafia Princess

* Can't Leave Him Alone After the Love Made

* Meet Me at the Altar

***

FACEBOOK.COM:

@AUTHOROLIVIASHAW

INSTAGRAM:

@MRSOLIVIAWRITES

CPSIA information can be obtained
at www.ICGtesting.com
Printed in the USA
LVHW04s1031040618
579499LV00004B/461/P